Grey All Over

Grey All Over

Andrea Actis

Brick Books

Library and Archives Canada Cataloguing in Publication

Title: Grey all over / Andrea Actis.
Other titles: Gray all over
Names: Actis, Andrea, 1984- author.
Description: Poems.
Identifiers: Canadiana (print) 20200389459 | Canadiana (ebook) 20200389467 | ISBN 9781771315395 (softcover) | ISBN 9781771315401 (HTML) | ISBN 9781771315418 (PDF)
Classification: LCC PS8601.C85 G74 2021 | DDC C811/.6—dc23

We acknowledge the Canada Council for the Arts, the Government of Canada through the Canada Book Fund, and the Ontario Arts Council for their support of our publishing program.

Canada Council for the Arts Conseil des arts du Canada Canada ONTARIO ARTS COUNCIL CONSEIL DES ARTS DE L'ONTARIO

The book is set in Adobe Caslon Pro.
Cover design by Emma Allain.
Interior design by Andrea Actis and Marijke Friesen.
Printed and bound by Coach House Printing.

Brick Books
487 King St. W.
Kingston, ON
K7L 2X7

www.brickbooks.ca

For my dead dad

CONTENTS

sort of like a déjà vu in reverse

Q, change dramatically - someone not good for you (male) confirmed

10-2808 Andrea Actis "cross over"

- very close 23 Pittman St. funny (where's his glasses) Healthiest happy, joyous free

talking was difficult at times Providence, R.I. 02906

↓ still knew how you felt

Beautiful deep colors - In spirit

(Purples - spirituality - spiritual) (3) 3 animals

(Blacks) "Gifts" good taste good things M

No rain - no rainbows

Coco Chanel Not cheap "see each other" and animal

"Now you're listening" "Hear this" relation w/ the 3 animals in spirit

w/ you - thinks you're the owner present - "240"

In spirit

- difficulty breathing or oxygen

- eyes/vision

- unconscious before going

"disturbing" - making a point (motion with the hands)

ring being committed

Strong - still strong (- 4 2 7)

"It just doesn't make sense"

trying to get your attention

Airplanes - flew or scared of it

"You couldn't have paid me to fly" - sigh -

"You're safe"

you're tense - "You need to relax"

"Walking difficult"

(Duquesne University) Tammy / Hammy / Tammies (talking is a little different)

Tamberrans - heritage - where you came from

"Work with the hands - that is good"

Old schooled - He's just as smart" - a smile on his face

SOUL ASH

And you know you get everybody you want in there. And you can keep it and spread it. Yet I feel that somehow this might be just having no material parts of them. Like a really smart person making the argument for her. So then that's blinded by *his* belief that it is soul to these people? So very. Dispersed. But what sense slews why soul might simply be what I remember of someone and love of them? I remind her why my love no I don't have investments I'm looking to protect them.

Well truly I think it is something that you cannot really measure in this present. The soul is something that is going to be eased upon death that goes back to how it goes back really goes. Goes into this whatever this plasticine this kind of playdough kids use. So it's going to be fun again to be some other persons. Like is going to be transmitted and you should get a really big chunk of oh my. In their sadness or even health or what have you. See in the future it's not you it's not me. You might actually resemble Jeffrey just because by chance you took a piece of that playdough. But you know a well-defined shape? You know a random assimilation? You gotta be so so so good that that was truly the case no I *know* you put people in the drawer. You know gathering all kinds of ashes from people and giving them a line in a drawer in your apartment.

Though I don't even think this is a question of metaphysics or like what's actually real. I think that there might be something if we look at just this behavioral pattern of gathering and displaying ash right. That there might be telling in a way? Like I'm not imagining that in fact we were throwing souls in this purgatory and they mean Jeffrey Mona Marti. There are not some screaming like ahhhhhhhhh you're keeping me from the big waterslide in the sky! It is not that bad. The fact that you know there is this holding on is just exactly what this is. That this is ancestor. But the idea that you're holding them basically on the phone that you don't release them from the thing is disgusting to me even if you release some finger of them on the mountaintop or whatever. You are really a part of the hoarding. You're like still holding on to part of ash and so on to make it garbage in your apartment. So this isn't nice. And that's hello why I object.

Well thank you at least for saying to me because you to me have this interesting hybrid belief like very hard science and some scared-shitless form of Catholicism that makes you an Eastern European man. You study the brain but don't understand what this brain is doing to how you argue with me. Then it's like that is *so* not how long I will always keep a little bit of the view that I was going to cremate. You will die! What will happen to ashes afterwards? I don't even care I will go into the stupid cupboard with them in my apartment. I don't even care what happens there or what happens exactly to match those ashes. No not yours but them and those.

I just don't understand why this is the question of the evening because we have like four actual people here. One two three four whatever whatever parts. I say that the four of us is this could be our grief currently talking? We're looking for like object substitutes you know but even then I still think me and my mind are better at the seriousness now freaking *learn* what they are. Excuse me? Because me and my mom are better at listening to souls and not forgetting what exactly some people were? Now that's what I'm saying.

What I'm saying is just that you and I both right now we're looking at like palm prints of Mona Lisa from when she dies. She's like I am this trace this real *Wheaten Terrier* and we're both exactly enchanted at this. The object that has about this strange index equality is there in dusty chunk in the kitchen. It's an impression of this moment it reminds us of this moment that was absolutely true that will probably in time if mourning doesn't work become less true you know this moment of just losing the beloved poof. And right now that isn't simply a fucked-up version of hey I'm assessing blame to you. These ashes are soul for them Andrea. So what would be if you died in three years gone? What is going to happen to those issues that you're so preciously hiding in the bottom of your drawer and whatnot? How can you take responsibility for all those ashes all those souls when you actually lose control? How will cash be a thing for you when you fail?

Can you please yell more quietly? No I'm sorry it's late but this is fully to you. Well I didn't like your explanation it was like a factual story of who you are but it's not what I'd call an *argumentum*. Okay so the depths of imagining death for our family people is that a lot? You know I'm like no. But to think that I say to you permission for everything? No for nope I don't. I've *met* everything. I actually would do very bad things to those ashes you know I might shit them out I might drink four wines and do some taking it to the beach without you. But you know the fact the fact is that I don't trust you with those ashes. Because they no because you're not doing the right thing to them right now. What is that even like for you?

What would be the right thing and the right thing to do to them would be to bury them all in just one place to get rid of all of this stuff that be kept in a drawer or whatever wherever you keep your part of Jeffrey Mona Marti that is a disgrace to them I think. What I would say is maybe that that would work. Yeah I'm interested in what you're telling in terms of like if I turned away here and just kept listening. So some random Hungarian man for the laws and protocols of assimilation? No I'm not gonna take it and just put them into the film box or whatever it is in Burnaby Mountain. And you still have parts of the ashes somewhere. Yeah in your possession but you need to put them *all* in there where it is finally not for your possession. That's what I'm saying. Don't keep a small something in your drawer superstition right? What do you think I say?

I cannot sleep. She cannot split ashes. It's what I'm saying that there's no such thing as the whole of ash. Why? Insofar as turning a body into ash is already an incalculable transformation. Yes it is but on the other hand you don't know exactly what happens to this yeah *nobody nobody* knows that. I agree with this so strongly in one thing because nobody nobody knows what happens when you finally go sky but you'll see that I strongly disapprove your way about it. There is a church market for that. Yeah okay so be it. Ashes and the collection of ashes. And here I'm still a little sensitive. Hang on to your own ashes then but it's very bad magic. Well actually who knows? It's so much bigger than you and you your arrogance it fascinates me.

I just feel like boys don't really know what you see here. Though you both have something to say to each other it seems to me and I feel like I'm maybe a third party to this telling. I don't *have* any ashes. But for come forward at least and say as Croatian witch will you tell us exactly what is bad about ashes? Just say it. Okay it's nothing about ashes it's just so wrong to keep parts. Andrea doesn't understand this tiny little bit of truth no I actually just have a different definition of wholeness. As ash like for any sand it *is* soul. What's vital is saying it has some resonance some playdough vibration and maybe you are guilty of a limited seriousness with it. Then it's like well what if we you just fear holding on this purple memory without history? Like how does an ash get caught become sign?

I just question to use a piece of the ash. That's correct. But once you're fully immersed in the materials you hear things like oh I'm inhaling atoms that were once a part of Shakespeare's body and everything is so radically intermingled. You always do that CO_2 to actually form a Shakespeare we inhale. So in that sense. Like the ashes are. It doesn't matter whether we have them they're already gone and back and here again and even if we threw them away shit them out they'd be right into us anyway. So all we're talking about is the ritual. Do I want to preserve this substance that has a name? Because ash is just ash right and calling it like oh this is Jeffrey is insane. Right? No it's both insane and not insane. It can be a beautiful phenomenon when you do that.

I mean that's why it's holy because it's like this is clearly not my dad is just the little opal weed vessel. This is why I think that we should not tell each other what to do with it because it's just so soul sucking to argue with me like this. I always had my own take on this. Sure you have your own take on this but basically you know the souls of these people rest on your shoulder. Except no I don't buy that. What would I even take from your shoulder? Well what Andrea said about wholeness I think is an important mention. It's so if you want to have the ritual of how to cook the grief quickly instead of doing things piecemeal finding within yourself some type of like whole ghost gesture might be important. It gets defined as *oh we need to embalm the body or burn the body or put the body completely in*. So certainty. But that's all we can do or something right?

There was this fellow in England you know where it was like apparently very easily easy become a funeral director there. And he decided that he was going to start having MDMA funerals. So everyone in attendance would take MDMA and you would say farewell to your beloved deceased with him in that way. But it wasn't just like *oh MDMA* yeah but why is it always some kind of extraterrestrial drug that you have to ingest? You know you know just have a fun time at the funeral drink eat. Why extraterrestrial drug? He just thought that it permitted a type of openness that allows for a deeper acknowledgement. What interests me isn't the MDMA it was the following bit that's the falling prescription which assumed dogmatic status. And it was you have to see the body. You have to see it maybe touch it. And I don't know how I stand with regard to that!

I mean that is a part of the Roman Catholic and it's a part of the Reform you know is part of the ceremony that you actually have to crawl to see inside the coffin. In fact one of these you have to go and kiss. Exactly. But why to elevate and elevate and close? Well as long as you keep using your drawer I have a different worry for you completely. I'm not religious but I be richer and I think I know that today and forever. So you can keep all these ashes in your drawer and I'll be against it till the day I die. You know there's no excuse for this.

Sorry no excuse for what? I thought you said I had an excuse my excuse is I disagree with you. Is that what I said? You letting me off the hook. No letting off hook! I really don't see this is the case for keeping the ashes. I completely dispute with you. No I don't need your comments I don't need any body comments. I am precise. No that's not what I say. I'm sorry but wait twenty minutes ago you suggesting we put all of ash rations together in the film box. As long as it was all of them as well as all of them. They should all be together I say because you cannot take from or add to something in your apartment.

Well look I was saying that to close I agree closure is important. Closure is really really important. And I think that you guys are both completely agreed on that that closure no we don't is important. I emphasize this. I just don't want to see my relatives' ashes in a drawer. I want peace. I don't want peace. I'm honouring them. Oh yeah? I mean I don't think that there would be objection on their part I think they're quite okay with these the pragmatics of intuition or whatever. But the question is also like what is the most effective means of finding closure? How about opening?

I think you're right that having an effective and special ritual is key. Yeah. I find it feeling lest the wound to be open perpetually and at the expense of your ability to lives. And so that's basically what I say that you know I have some hope. Yeah I mean I mean I mean that as long as parts of the ashes scattered around in various drawers of Andrea cannot be at an ease you don't even know what exactly is resting. You are sitting in some drawers maybe somewhere whatever. But I mean I would imagine that that is just hard to be at ease with loss period. Yeah I know you didn't go through you didn't have to quite navigate so much the haunting still I know you can reach these deaths. I mean as opposed to alienated I feel that somehow there's a connection to those ashes. But it doesn't do for that what the problem is. Andrea she doesn't see that.

She's keeping the ashes well. But you have to ask yourself and Andrea has to ask herself what she is keeping from *us*. I mean that's why I think what you're saying is fascinating because it's like you know how the hell do we process these things that are just truly impossible and truly are? I don't know if I've dealt adequately with the laws of entities for my life. And that's what you have to think. You must grow up and face. But it did that there's an adequate verb to respect and acknowledge and continue to live with.

You have to ask you know does she ever dream of them or never feel guilty? I can't answer that on her behalf as she talks about them and thinks about them and communes with them and loves them. Oh really? And I would think that that that is supreme because it's like I mean I guess I'm maybe just a selfish materialist. Not that I deny that there's anything like an eternity of the soul or of its energies and needs that persist in the mountaintop. But I guess I'm certainly aware that the living preserved the dead via possibly their drawer in their apartment. And when I see that love my first concern is like it's not it's actually not for the well-being of the cash it's for me and for us and for doing and listening better. Like how is that living person coping with but not closing the loss? I mean also yeah. That's fine. Just like as you say an eternal combustion. Time to go to go and take care of her. To take your magnesium. Sorry totally. Well fine. Goodnight.

I am going to bed.
I am goiNG BeD
This is my
Dad.
DAD
12
11
1
10
2
9
3
8
4
5

DOES ANDREA DREAM OF ELECTRIC DEAD

02:23

one video of an old simon and garfunkel concert -- happen to notice David at the end, leaning against the stage, them me and Brandon as small kids beside him. thisin tandem with another video-? pippi lingstoxkin, I am the little brunette and everyone is amazed. theres another video but I forget now...feel strongly like I need to warn Brandon about something...dad has something to do with things but I Dover what,,, wake up with a thinking/feeling he is alive, then remember...somehow almost not sure whether I myself am alive or dead, a hundred or just 234 now.

Driver's Daily Log
Lemons' & Greg's
x cellent
Adventure!

04:39

i was hanging with dad after finally reaching him on the phone. had tried several times (on his bday, Xmas), and he acted like "oh, I hadn't realized." a little upset by his blitheness, but was happy to see him anywasy. then got a reply about something to do with money from Vera. she was totally defensive and had no willingness to understand the appeal of my email. then I saw a newspaper clipping, a kind of lifestyle feature page, with her and Michael seated in lawnchairs in Newport or sinfully. a whole interview about how they'd tried so hard to help me and family (even my dad! apparently theyd had him over for dinner recently and it wasn't so bad, he'd bought a new pair of "wranglers, we believe?" for the occasion,..of course he hadn't mentioned any of this to me). but now they'd given up, been hurt by the poor arm of the family too many times, but at least they had each other and their love that is such a good love! finally dad admitted to me that he hadn't been in touchy because he'dd been too depressed. no surprise there. then somehow we were down by the water and making our way up a grassy hill to Vera and Michael's property. there were some beautifully ripe strawberries near the house that I discouraged him from picking because they struck me as totally gross or not worth it given whose house they were growing beside. woke up as I was trying to compose and email or texts to Vera denying a bunch of lies shed accuses me of ((including pretending not to know that they'd so generouzly had my dad over for dinner..)...ready to cut everyone not-poor out of my life entirely.

01:54

dad was back and thankfully ate all the accumulated panettone, even though it was summer and i ddidn't have anything except Earth Balance to put on it. he tried to tell me that lie again about how when a girffafe sits down it cannot ever get up without having a heart attack.

03:28

dad got a job managing a call-in customer service center for Internet network stuff ??. had been don by the water/dock with some new birds I was going to domesticate -- two little finches red and blue, who died, and a green and a blue budgie, who were adoriable and didn't die. knew i was going to meet dad up in the hill for lunch, so was happy. sort of a cross between edmonton and penetanguishine (sp?). make my way towards dad's work and when I get there he's in the thick of it, on a headset and swivel chair being all star trekand really seeming to enjoy it since he's always known he's an alien or at least has met aliens. I get a chance to sneak a peek at incoming customer ratings online and they're all mentioning how great and helpful this new Jeffrey is (vs. some other "eastern INdian man" who worked there.. haha fuck..,mustve gotten that from risperdal drug forum troll yesterday?). and deep inside I know dads not drinking and has a good chance of not starting again because he knows he's good at this and there are no toxic fumes etc. alarm goes off before we are able to head out to lunch, but all the feelings are positive and I am very proud of him.

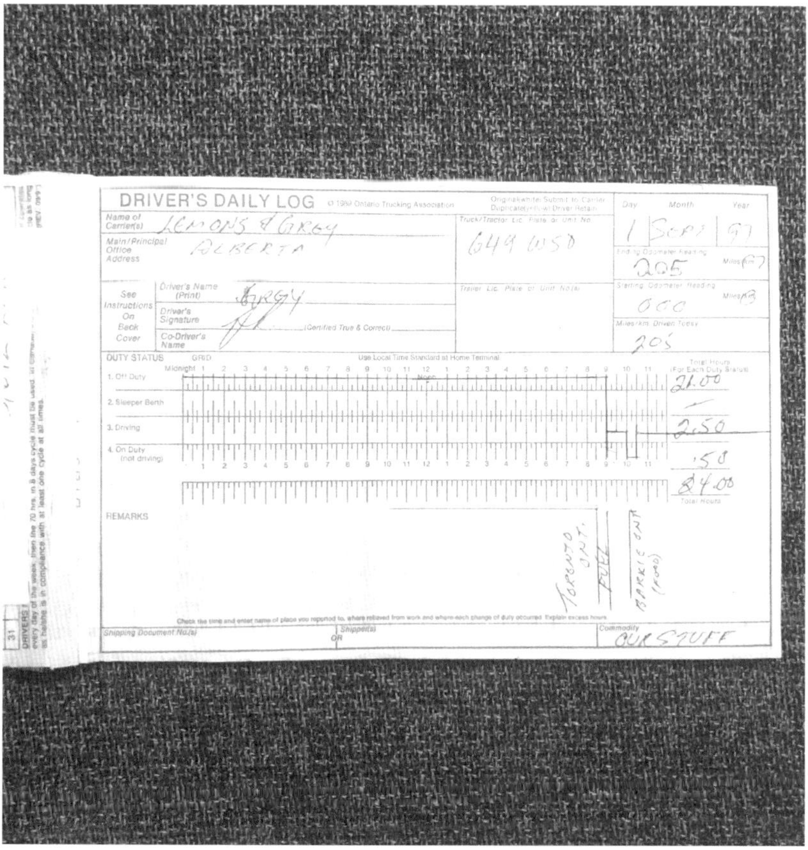

DRIVER'S DAILY LOG © 1989 Ontario Trucking Association

Original(white) Submit to Carrier
Duplicate(yellow) Driver Retain

Day	Month	Year
1	SEPT	97

Name of Carrier(s): LEMONS & GRGY

Main/Principal Office Address: ALBERTA

Truck/Tractor Lic. Plate or Unit No.: 649 WSD

Ending Odometer Reading: 205 Miles/km

Starting Odometer Reading: 000 Miles/km

Miles/km Driven Today: 205

See Instructions On Back Cover

Driver's Name (Print): GRGY

Driver's Signature: (Certified True & Correct)

Co-Driver's Name

Trailer Lic. Plate or Unit No(s)

DUTY STATUS — GRID — Use Local Time Standard at Home Terminal

Midnight 1 2 3 4 5 6 7 8 9 10 11 12 Noon 1 2 3 4 5 6 7 8 9 10 11

Total Hours (For Each Duty Status)

Duty Status	Total Hours
1. Off Duty	21.00
2. Sleeper Berth	—
3. Driving	2.50
4. On Duty (not driving)	.50
Total Hours	24.00

REMARKS

TORONTO ONT.

FUEL

BARRIE ONT (FORD)

Check the time and enter name of place you reported to, where relieved from work and where each change of duty occurred. Explain excess hours.

Shipping Document No(s) OR Shipper(s)

Commodity: OUR STUFF

31 DRIVERS — every day of the week, then the 70 hrs. in 8 days cycle must be used ... as he/she is in compliance with at least one cycle at all times.

2:03

don't really remember now! dad was present, but there was some vague sense that we were sad about when he wouldnt be and he knew he was leaving too. that autexhew song I used to listen to a lot was playing and made it seem like we were at a rave but better thanost eaves.

04:12

I'm terminally ill. a brain tumor caused by a bladder infection ?. I and everyone in the family (dad's gona already) know I'm going to pass by the end of the day. I'm sobbings and scared, but able to take comfort in knowing that if someone as close to me and so funny and sensitive as jeff has actually been through the death dance than I can go through the death dance too. I try to explain ot mom and marti and tata but they are so fucked up and have totally forgotten how to speak English.

06:17

first day of grad school, Dad drives me in the red avn or white truck and of course I've fuckoing arranged for him to sit in on the class. I'm in the centre front fow, he's in the back. I know he's there the whole time. I feel him listening, engaging, even though the proff is peter Popoff and he class is so- so. I think it's on some kind of eco- or even traidiontally/ aristocratically botanical topic. I sense he's going to leave, and he does. he gets up and quietly slips out of the room. I feel I won't see him again that day. then my mom slips into the room. the topic and teacher change to comupters/ infoeteach stuff (kind of a chiasmic theme/vocation switcharoo for the two o them.) and a Jamaican professor with birhgt ried lipstick. my mom sits in the back of the room for the durection af the lecture, pretending to understand and sort of mimicking the woman's gestures and looking my way for approval. afterwards my mom asks th e woman if she wants to come out dancing with us and i am super pissed off/embarrassed/ disappointed.

05:21

living in an house with greatgrandmother Mimi and Rachel jones and that Tommy person who used to live the basement. doing some drinking, steal a beer and a bittle of wine for sleeptimme then pass out on the unmade bed with fresh sheets. Rachaela, after freaking out at Jason about something, flies into me room and then notices the beer and wine. totally flips her lid and I feel betrayed and tiny. screaming at eachother. i yell no wonder I turned out better than you kid did! and she goes oh yeah well your dad ABUSED you. i freAk out and run upstairs passing silent 96 year old mimi who's standing at the top. mostly naked I run out of the house into the snowy night and then suddenly rethink what i'm doing in light of mimi's presence and feelings. go back inside and she seems so relieved and I bend over and hug her very tight and say I love her.. noticing her smells and the paperiness of her cheek which I'm against and kissing. I think, you knows, i had the good grace of being half-this family,, and also of remembering this in my self destructive moments and impulses that scare everyone, letting love and calm win over, OK, it's totally okay and truthful to not rage..?,also Mimi as my caregiver who I taught to say "helicopter" while watching Die HArd having real witness and access to the truth of my dad's love and sacrifice for me. how she loved Jeffrey too. all this getting me towarda waking up. almost decided not to write this down!

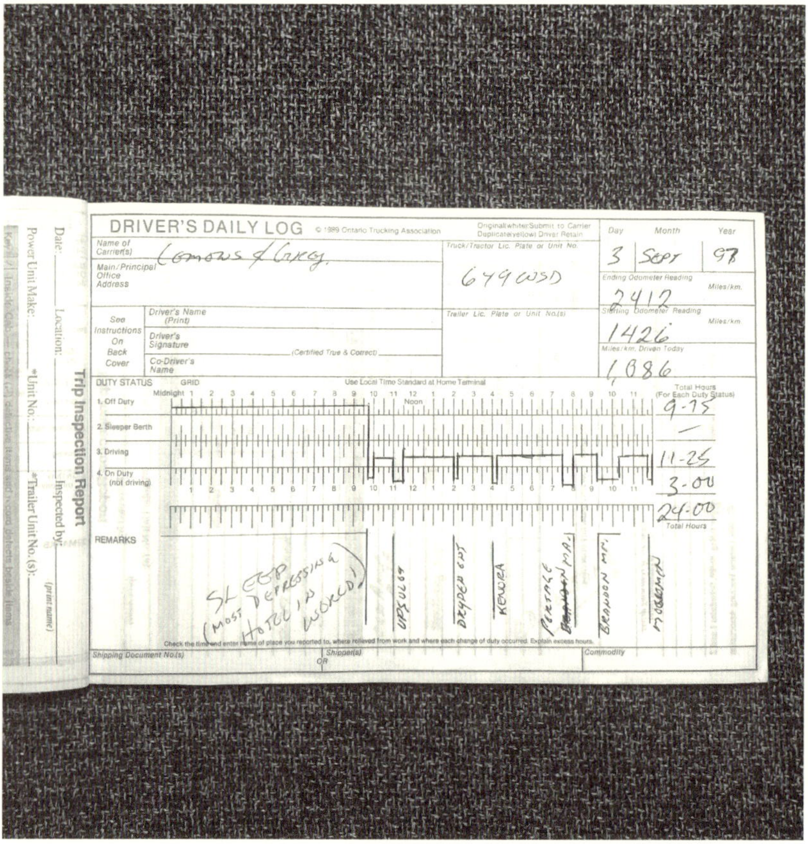
DRIVER'S DAILY LOG
© 1989 Ontario Trucking Association
Original(white)Submit to Carrier
Duplicate(yellow) Driver Retain
Day 3
Month SEPT
Year 97
Name of Carrier(s) Lemons & Greg
Main/Principal Office Address
Truck/Tractor Lic. Plate or Unit No. 679 WSD
Ending Odometer Reading 2412 Miles/km.
Starting Odometer Reading 1426 Miles/km
Miles/km. Driven Today 1,086
See Instructions On Back Cover
Driver's Name (Print)
Driver's Signature
(Certified True & Correct)
Co-Driver's Name
Trailer Lic. Plate or Unit No.(s)
DUTY STATUS
GRID
Use Local Time Standard at Home Terminal
Midnight
Noon
Total Hours (For Each Duty Status)
1. Off Duty 9-75
2. Sleeper Berth —
3. Driving 11-25
4. On Duty (not driving) 3-00
24-00
Total Hours
REMARKS
SLEEP (MOST DEPRESSING HOTEL IN WORLD!)
UPSULA
DRYDEN ONT
KENORA
PORTAGE BRANDON MA.
BRANDON MA.
MOOSOMIN
Check the time and enter name of place you reported to, where relieved from work and where each change of duty occurred. Explain excess hours.
Shipping Document No.(s)
Shipper(s)
OR
Commodity
Trip Inspection Report
Date:
Location:
Inspected by:
(print name)
Power Unit Make:
*Unit No.:
*Trailer Unit No.(s):

03:33

dad and I in the Pony heading east along Hastings, around Slcoan, with McDonalds chicken sandwiches in our hands, him a Mchiskne, nme a crispy chicken. I seruosly didn't wantone but I knew he wanted one and wouldn'tta ve stopped if I hadn't wanted one too. I hold mine as he eats his and complains/stresses out about things. I'm feeling stressed out by his stress. he's worried about money, his landlord, etc. cloudy and heavy out. whole scene like the day in real life where for no reason (not even wednesdapy!) we stopped for Whoppers and enjoyed the fucking shit out of them --ecept not AS happy).

05:42

I'm renewing some kind of citizenship or studentship forms for myself, a process requiringthe at I present my mom's Romanian passports (she hads many??).they Re expired, I tell him, but hope they'll be okay! he makes an obvious horehound exception , dramatically as through if it weren't for his kindness I woo have to go back to Atlantis or whareever. he takes the documentation, after which he opens the largest binder and flips to the section 100% about my family. it's all photos of my dad, though--cut out around his various silhouettes like val would have done to the photos she was goof to collage (before Photoshop). these wrt photos id never seen before, thought most were from whatever afternoon it was when he ware that stained mauve sweatshirt and the dark cap (in Kelowna I think, the day we drove into town and back, remarking on the new UBC pkanagam campus and then eating so many hot wings at the pub at the bottom tf the hill). he is making a few clowny happy poses in the photos, excitedly waving shadows and huge hands and infuckong miss him!

02:57

we're moving dad's stuff, he doesn't want to move. sits lookrjn horribly sad in the chair that always breaks with like old gummy bears stuck on the cushion. he doesn't have much stuff but it still somehow takes us eight years to move. we know eight years have passed because of some fancy eclipse or "transit" or whatever that is now happening, but we don't run outside to watch because we know if we let him out of our sgeht he will disappear from us. his sweaters keep changing and at a certain point he is wearing some of the kid sweatshisfd I used to have--don't worry be happy sweatshirt, bart simpson, generic jazz dancer girls, puffy paint, Milli vanilla, glow in the dark vegetables. I say he looks stupid in them and for a seconf amd scared he is going to blow his brains out at my comment but then thank god he laughs, and so does everyone but he still doesn't want to move.

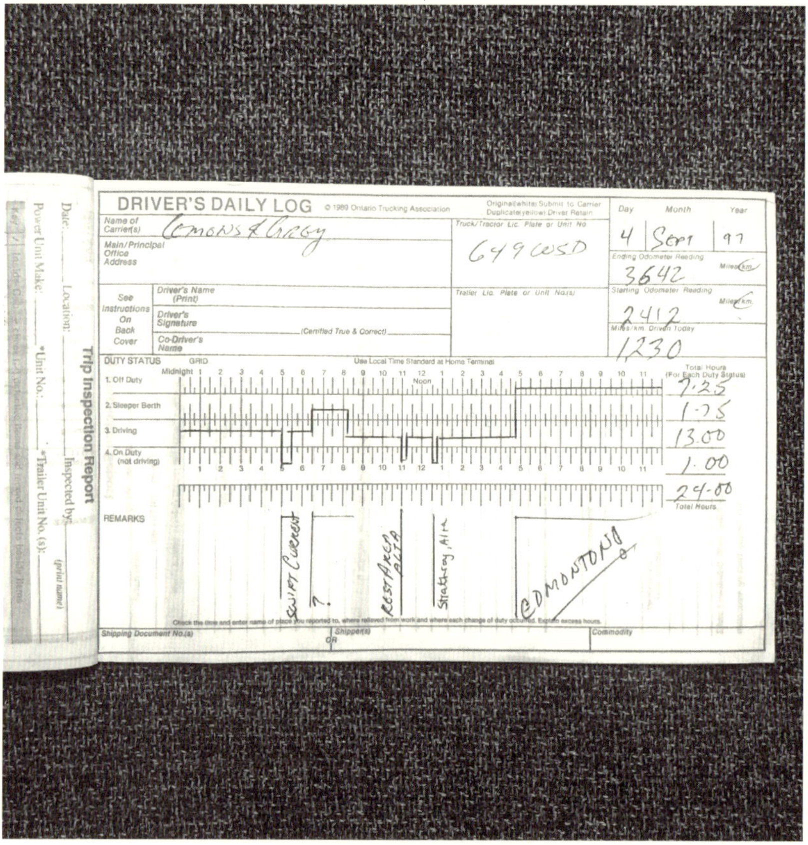

Trip Inspection Report

Date: ______ Location: ______ Inspected by: ______ (print name)

Power Unit Make: ______ *Unit No.: ______ *Trailer Unit No. (s): ______

DRIVER'S DAILY LOG © 1989 Ontario Trucking Association

Original(white) Submit to Carrier
Duplicate(yellow) Driver Retain

Day	Month	Year
4	Sept	97

Name of Carrier(s): Lemons & Grey

Main/Principal Office Address

Truck/Tractor Lic. Plate or Unit No: 649 WSD

Ending Odometer Reading: 3642 Miles/km

Starting Odometer Reading: 2412 Miles/km

Miles/km Driven Today: 1230

See Instructions On Back Cover

Driver's Name (Print)

Driver's Signature (Certified True & Correct)

Co-Driver's Name

Trailer Lic. Plate or Unit No.(s)

DUTY STATUS GRID — Use Local Time Standard at Home Terminal

Midnight 1 2 3 4 5 6 7 8 9 10 11 Noon 1 2 3 4 5 6 7 8 9 10 11

Duty Status	Total Hours (For Each Duty Status)
1. Off Duty	7.25
2. Sleeper Berth	1.75
3. Driving	13.00
4. On Duty (not driving)	1.00
Total Hours	24.00

REMARKS

Swift Current

Rest Area Alta

Strathroy, Alta

Edmonton

Check the time and enter name of place you reported to, where relieved from work and where each change of duty occurred. Explain excess hours.

Shipping Document No.(s) | Shipper(s) OR | Commodity

06:37

I guess we are roommates or something, and he says he is goint o get some milk at the gas station, be back in three minusa. but I KNOW there is something wrong, like is fefinitedly going off somewhere to die because he doesn't want to do it front of me (like any normal almost-dead person, that is their choice most typically). I beg him not to go and say "who needs milk!" but then he reminds me of how much I love to dip my Pirate cookies in them. fine. so three minutes are up and I put on my bathrobe and go out looking for him. next thing I know I am back in the apartment, it smells like fried eggs, the air is smoky and red but pleasant, and I know he is gone. I breathe deeply in the way therapists death you to breathe and decide to hold off calling mom and marti and tat.a . then I approach a narrow wicker hutch that ddidnt used tobe there, and spend the rest of the dream inspecting and engaging with all the new items that have been left on it: all the stuff that was in dad's room when he died and that I still hae---boken reading glasses, paint covered cellphne, pom pom cigar butt, half a mickey of st. remy, some of a snickers bar, gummy worms, Panama mug, Penske hat, etca0 --but also new even weirder stuff, like some teeth and pubes. oh well, it's still him, and it's good to have these things!

04:18

I'm in a suicide pact with some boy and some girl. sort of an 'on the beach' situation. university hill figures somehow (like we were going to do it after the milk run?) . then my dad comes along ((or has possibly been our gym teacher all this thyme)and goes, "one suicide of mine counts for three suicides of yours!: and of course the other two are like "Sweet! off the hjook;" but I am so upset and can't stop crying because I know he's going to do it and it still hurts even though the apocalypse is coming soon or at least we fuckonng wish it were coming to let us everyone off the hook also it's alredy here anyas.

Peter Popoff P.O. Box 760 Upland, CA 91785

UPLAND
NOV 19 '01
CA

0.85
U.S. POSTAGE
PB METER 7103308

Jeffrey Actis
10191 5 Rd
Richmond, BC CANADA V7A 4E4

Jeffrey,
This letter contains important Revelations...

00101+3407

Jeffrey our prayer center received your phone call... I have been praying on your behalf non-stop ever since the operator gave me your name. **Jeffrey Actis, did I spell that correctly?** When you called perhaps you thought it was by accident... I feel that A HIGHER POWER directed you to call. **I HAVE SOMETHING IMPORTANT TO TELL YOU... SO PLEASE READ ON.**

Jeffrey Actis
10191 5 Rd
Richmond, BC CANADA V7A 4E4

November 14, 2001

Dear Jeffrey, it is not unusual for God to send those with "HARD CASES" to me.

No disrespect to anyone... but in my spirit I feel you've tried to get help before, but to no avail. Many are not anointed to deal with "DIFFICULT CASES". Perhaps this anointing is so strong upon me **because** I have PERSONALLY overcome some of the same challenges you are now facing in my own life.

Jeffrey, in my prayer time, **God showed me some of the "HARD THINGS"** you are now dealing with. God gave me this word for you... *"FEAR NOT, MY Son, Jeffrey, THE "HARD THINGS" YOU ARE NOW FACING WILL SOON BE A THING OF THE PAST... FOR DURING THE NEXT SEVERAL MONTHS I WILL USE MY PROPHET TO LEAD THEE INTO DELIVERANCE... AND REVEAL UNTO THEE THE STEPS OF FAITH THAT WILL BREAK ALL EVIL HOLDS ON YOUR life AND RELEASE MIRACLES OF LOVE, SUCCESS, NEW HEALTH AND JOYOUS LIVING UNTO THEE."* **Well, as you can see you have made the right new contact.**

IMPORTANT: Notice the sealed envelope... DO NOT OPEN IT JUST YET... the packet of water you requested is inside... and... also a powerful prophecy for you.

But FIRST you must read this entire letter: Jeffrey Actis, By God's direction I've undertaken this assignment of defeating these "HARD THINGS" in your life that are now holding you back... I am so certain that as you OBEY GOD IN FAITH... **YOU WILL ACHIEVE SUCCESS AND GET THE RESULTS YOU WANT WITH GOD'S HELP.** *The faith in my heart is saying to you, Jeffrey Actis, during the next few weeks you can become prosperous, more joyous than ever before, understand and know your future, and live a life filled to overflowing with love and happiness.*

I took your name, anointed it and commanded evil spirits... to bow to the Power of Almighty God. In Jesus' Name, I speak to witchcraft and all evil and command it to recede.

THROUGH THIS MIGHTY TIME OF PRAYER... The Grace and Favor of God has been restored to you... **BUT,** we must work to restore the power, peace, health and prosperity that satan has stolen from you. **God revealed to me in an awesome, SECRET VISION... things that I MUST SHARE with you at this time.**

(Jeffrey, please read on.)

YOUR SECRET WAY TO A LIFE OF ABUNDANCE

No matter how dark your situation is now I believe God is going to show you the way to health, a life of abundance and supernatural power that He has already ordained to you. Perhaps no one can see it right now, but God has prepared the way.

*Together **WE WILL...**
- ask for God's help with prayer.
- *expect God to uncover His road
- through your "Red Sea" situation.
- *Release our faith in obedience to his leading.

*Go forward and cross over and into your Promised Land! Let the miracles begin!

*Jeffrey, I believe God has a SECRET WAY THAT ONLY HE CAN SEE (right now) through your problems and troubled waters that lead into a life of total VICTORY and ABUNDANCE. USE YOUR PACKET OF MIRACLE SPRING WATER AS I INSTRUCTED AND THEN COMPLETE THIS PRAYER SHEET AND GET IT BACK TO ME TODAY! I'm going to release a prophet's anointing for you! I believe that the Holy Spirit wants to uncover your pathway to MIRACLE VICTORY!

WRITE YOUR SECRET WAY MIRACLE REQUEST BELOW

I NEED GOD TO MAKE A WAY IN THE FOLLOWING AREAS OF MY LIFE:

CHECK:

( ) FINANCES ( ) SPECIAL PERSONAL NEED ____________

( ) MARRIAGE

( ) JOB/CAREER ____________

( ) HEALTH

( ) SPIRIT & MIND ____________

( ) MY CHILDREN

( ) OTHER ____________

*IMPORTANT

MY LOVEDONES NAME: ____________ THEIR RELATIONSHIP TO ME: ____________

THEIR NEEDS: ____________

Jeffrey, now release your faith through your giving. LET THIS BE YOUR FIRST STEP FORWARD AND ACROSS YOUR RED SEA SITUATION AND INTO YOUR HEALTHY, PROSPEROUS, JOYOUS FUTURE.

( ) PETER, I AM MOVING FORWARD... IN JESUS' NAME, BY FAITH!

HERE IS MY GIFT OF LOVE, FAITH AND OBEDIENCE TO GOD THAT I HAVE ANOINTED --

AMOUNT ENCLOSED ( ) $ 27.00 ( ) OTHER $____________

( ) PLEASE SEND ME YOUR FREE NEW BOOK "PROSPERITY THINKING".

Jeffrey Actis
10191 5 Rd
Richmond, BC CANADA V7A 4E4

518755

Jeffrey,

I really believe GOD IS ABOUT TO LEAD YOU INTO A WHOLE NEW LIFE! What you have to do is use what FAITH YOU HAVE... NO MATTER HOW SMALL IT MAY SEEM TO YOU. Are you facing a hard situation and having a DIFFICULT TIME making a decision to cross over the "RED SEA" WATERS OF YOUR LIFE? I feel you already know in your heart that GOD WILL HEAL AND DELIVER YOU... But you have not yet stepped out completely in faith. I BELIEVE THIS IS YOUR DAY. DO WHAT YOU CAN AND GOD WILL DO THE REST.

Love, Peter

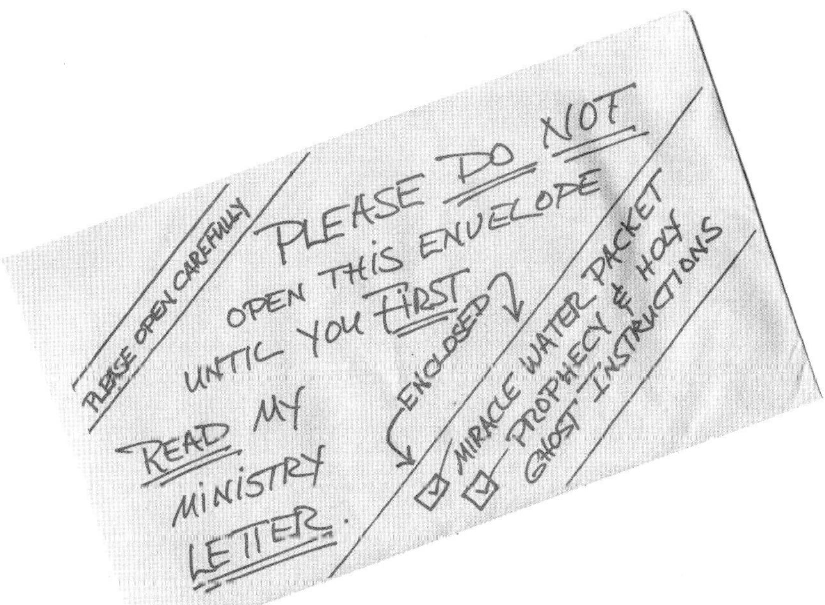
PLEASE OPEN CAREFULLY
PLEASE DO NOT
OPEN THIS ENVELOPE
UNTIL YOU FIRST
READ MY
MINISTRY
LETTER.
ENCLOSED
MIRACLE WATER PACKET
PROPHECY & HOLY
GHOST INSTRUCTIONS

MIRACLE
SPRING
WATER

TUESDAY

1) CALL ADDICTION SERVICES MAPLE RIDGE : 604 467 5179 (830-430 closed 12-100 for lunch)
[2477 Lougheed Hwy @ 225th St. across from Dairy Queen]
- tell them you want A referral to A RESIDENTIAL TREATMENT CENTRE and to be put ON A wait list.

* Addiction Services Vancouver contact Jo ANNE 604 215 3990

2) FIND A FAMILY DOCTOR – CALL AROUND! GET AN APPOINTMENT A.S.A.P. → TELL THEM YOU were AT EMERGENCY RECENTLY AND DIDN'T GET ANY TREATMENT

In case of loss, please return to:

JEFF ACTIS.

778 235 4115

778 896 5931

As a reward: $

HAD A LOT OF CONVERSATION WITH ROBYN TODAY. SHE ASKED ME FOR MY NUMBER FOR HER LIST OF FRIENDS FROM HERE. PERHAPS I'LL TRY ATTENDING SOME MEETINGS WITH HER IN THE NEAR FUTURE. THERES A FEW PEOPLE HERE I'VE TAKEN A LIKING TOO THIS PAST WEEK; BUT I HAVE TO SAY ROBYN IS THE STAR. SUCH A GOOD HEART. SHE'S LEAVING SUNDAY AND I THINK SHE'S NOT SURE ABOUT THAT - I THINK THE STRESS OF HER EVERYDAY LIFE HAS BEGUN TO WEAR ON HER, AND THIS IS CERTAINLY HAD AN INFLUENCE ON HER ALCOHOL USE - HER ALCOHOL HABIT IS "A MICKY A NIGHT" - A PALTRY AMOUNT TO MINE REALLY - BUT - AS I'VE BEEN TOLD "I'LL HAVE A 'STRONG CONSTITUTION'" HEH. MAN - I CAN'T BELIEVE MYSELF THE AMOUNT OF REMY I'VE CONSUMED. FUCKING CRAZY. ANYWAY, I'LL MISS ROBYN WHEN SHE LEAVES, SHE'S A TOTAL SWEETHEART - I WISH HER ALL GOOD AND HAPPINESS. INTELLIGENCE, KINDNESS AND GOOD LOOKS ARE NOT OFTEN FOUND IN ONE, AND ROBYN HAS ALL OF THAT.

THE NEW TODAY BLONDE GIRL FREAKED OUT TODAY - TOLD EVERYONE TO SHUT UP THEY WERE TOO LOUD. I THINK SHE'S IN FOR A REALLY BAD TIME FOR A WHILE. SHE WAS OBVIOUSLY HIGH ON ARRIVAL SO HER

WITHDRAWAL WILL KICK IN TOMORROW. THE NEW ROOMIE - ROD - IS COOL. QUIET SPOKEN - HAS A BRAIN - GENTLE SNORING WHAT A RELIEF OVER THE LAST ONE. BEDTIME.

SATURDAY:

I SLEPT! SEVEN & ONE HALF HOURS. I REFUSED THE STUPID (SLEEP?) MEDS LAST NIGHT AND WAS GIVEN THE SAME THING I WAS FIRST GIVEN INSTEAD AND FINALLY SLEPT LIKE A STONE. SO, WHY THE HELL DID THEY MESS ME UP WITH THAT OTHER SHIT FOR TWO DAYS. I DON'T GET IT. "DESPITE ALL MY RAGE - I AM STILL JUST A RAT IN A CAGE"

ANYWAY - IT APPEARS JON IS BEING PUSHED OUT THE DOOR TODAY. SEEMS THE STAFF DIDN'T LIKE HIS LITTLE EPISODE WITH BLONDIES' PARTNER IN CRIME. ALSO, IT ALSO SEEMS THEY DIDN'T LIKE HIM SITTING SO CLOSE TO ROBYN LAST NIGHT. (NO INTIMACY ALLOWED.) THERE WILL BE A BIT OF A VOID HERE WHEN HE LEAVES. MORE THOUGHTS OF VAN KEASY. HE DOSEN'T STAND A CHANCE IN HELL OF NOT USING AGAIN (I GIVE HIM TWO DAYS

AT BEST). I'M PRETTY SURE ONE NEEDS MORE THAN FIVE DAYS TO SAY ADIOS TO HEROIN.

IT'S THE WEEKEND - NOT THAT IT MEANS ANYTHING IN PARTICULAR HERE. JUST THOUGHT I'D MENTION THAT.

BLONDIE LOOKS LIKE DEATH THIS MORNING - NO SURPRISE - BUT I'M SURPRISED TO SEE HER AWAKE THIS TIME OF DAY. (8:30 AM) I GUESS IT HAS'NT HIT HER YET.

I HOPE BREAKFAST IS EGGS & TOAST - SOMETHING OTHER THAN PASTRY TYPE THINGS. I'M NOT EATING ANY MORE SWEET BREADS AND PASTRIES. MAKES ME FAT AND ACIDY.

I'D SO LIKE TO SEE ANDREA. I MISS HER. ITS ONLY BEEN MAYBE TEN DAYS, BUT IF I THINK ABOUT IT, ITS BEEN A VERY LONG TIME THAT I'VE CHATTED WITH HER WITH A CLEAR-UNDISTURBED MIND. SHE'S COMPLETELY IMMERSED IN THESE FIVE PAPERS SHE NEEDS TO COMPLETE FOR DEC. 11. AND, AS ALWAYS, SHE HAS TO APPLY 110 PERCENT TO HER WORK. I SO ADMIRE HER DISCIPLINE AND DILIGENCE, BUT I DO STRESS A BIT OVER THE FACT THAT SHE APPLYS HER SELF SO HARD, AND IT WEARS HER OUT,

BUT [illegible], SHE'S YOUNG AND SEEMS
TO MANAGE. I'VE OFFERED, ON MANY
OCCASIONS, TO DO A PAPER OR TWO
FOR HER, JUST TO HELP - BUT SHE HAS
DECLINED. GO FIGURE - HEH.

EVERYONE - WELL NOT EVERYONE - BUT
THE CREW I'VE COME TO KNOW IS ASKING
FOR MY NUMBER. THEY TELL ME I'M
THE TYPE THAT MAY NEED A BIT OF
PRODDING, DRAGGING AND KICKING TO
MEETINGS; THEY'RE PROBABLY RIGHT.
EVERYONE IS LEAVING HERE WITH SUCH
GOOD INTENTIONS - I REALLY HOPE EVEN
HALF OF THEIR INTENTIONS MATERIALIZE.
THEY REALLY ARE DECENT PEOPLE. I STILL
KEEP THINKING WHAT A CRIME IT IS
TO JUST CUT EVERYONE LOOSE FROM
HERE. THERE'S THIS BIG EMPTY BUILDING
HERE - WHY NOT CENRTALIZE THIS WHOLE
PLACE - FROM DETOX TO TREATMENT ALL
UNDER ONE ROOF. IT MAKES SO MUCH
SENSE - I SUPPOSE TO MUCH SENSE
FOR THIS RIDICULOUS, WAYWARD
PROVINCIAL GOVERNMENT. IT'S
LIKE TUNNEL VISION.

BREAKFAST BECKONS.

OKAY - IT FALLS INTO PLACE. I HAVE
CONSTANTLY BEING REMINDED OF
THE KEASY STORY. THE CHARACTER IN
ONE FLEW OVER THE CUCKOO'S NEST

HIS NAME WAS 'MAC' IT'S APPARENT NOW, JON WAS MAC AROUND HERE

IT WILL BE DIFFERENT (AND QUIETER) AROUND HERE AS OF NOW. WISH HIM WELL.

I'VE BROWSED THROUGH A BIG BUNCH OF PAMPHLETS HERE - DIFFERENT OPTIONS FOR TREATMENT AVAILABLE UPON LEAVING HERE. (MOST FOR A LARGE COST) I JUST DON'T KNOW WHAT OR WHERE OR HOW? I FEEL A SAFE PLACE TO LIVE - AND THE OPPORTUNITY TO WORK OUT OF RESIDENCE IS DEFINITELY THE BEST COURSE FOR MYSELF. I REALLY BELIEVE THAT BEING ISOLATED IN A MEN'S ONLY SITUATION IS NOT A GOOD CHOICE FOR ME. I'VE SPENT MY ENTIRE LIFE SURROUNDED WITH FEMALES - I LIKE WOMENS COMPANY MUCH MORE THAN MOST MEN. AS I SEE IT, THE 'REAL' WORLD IS CO-ED. I THINK MEN & WOMEN GENERALLY, KEEP EACH OTHER FROM BEHAVING BADLY. JUST MY OPINION.

AFTERNOON GROUP IS PARTAKING IN THE DECORATING & SETTUP OF A CHRISTMAS TREE, ALL THE WHILE LISTENING TO XMAS CAROLS. THIS IS THE FIRST TIME SINCE MY ARRIVAL THAT I'VE REFUSED ANY "THERAPY" I FIND IT "ANTI-THERAPY" THE THOUGHT OF CHRISTMAS IN A PLACE

SUCH AS THIS IS COMPLETELY DEPRESSING. FOR ME, IF IT'S NOT FAMILY, IT'S NOT CHRISTMAS. THATS ALL I HAVE TO SAY ABOUT THAT.

I JUST SPOKE WITH ANDREA ON THE PHONE. SHE'S SOUNDS VERY STRESSED OUT - I'M NOT SURE IF IT COMES FROM THE WORKLOAD SHE'S UNDER - OR JUST THE FACT I, AND MY PREDICIMENT ARE MAKING HER UNEASY. I FEEL SHE'S AFRAID TO BE OPEN AND CANDID WITH ME; FEARING TO SOMEHOW INTERFERE WITH MY "CURE". I DO NOT WANT TO BE TREATED WITH 'KID GLOVES'. ME COMING HERE HAS, AS I KNEW IT WOULD, CHANGED THINGS. I ONLY HOPE FOR THE BETTER. FUCK. WHO'S TO KNOW WHAT THE RIGHT THING TO DO IS? WILL I BECOME SOMEONE NOBODY KNOWS? SOMEBODY I DON'T EVEN KNOW. SOMEBODY I DON'T EVEN LIKE? I DON'T KNOW, THE MORE I TRY TO MAKE SOME LOGICAL SENSE OF ALL THESE THOUGHTS - THE MORE OUT OF SORTS I BECOME.

JUST FINISHED AN AA MEETING (AGAIN) FOR SOME REASON (I THINK I'VE ALREADY SAID THIS) I FIND THE PEOPLE WITH AA MUCH MORE INTERESTING TO LISTEN TO.

MARTI & STEFAN DROPPED IN TO-NITE - WAS NICE TO SEE THEM. THEY ARE BEYOND AND ABOVE EVERYONE I'VE

EVER KNOWN. I SHALL ALWAYS LOVE THEM DEARLY. THEY MISTAKENLY BROUGHT A HUGE PAIL OF CIGARETTE TOBACCO AND A WHOLE CASE OF WHITE ZIG ZAG PAPERS – ENOUGH FOR TEN YEARS OF ROLLING. THEY ARE ADORABLE, AND HAVE BECOME THE PARENTS I NEVER HAD.

PEOPLE LEAVING TOMORROW – AL IS LEAVING – DECENT GUY THAT I PLAN AND HOPE TO CONTACT. ALSO, CUTE KARLA IS LEAVING – FIRST FOR HOME AND THEN TO THE TREATMENT CENTRE IN KELOWNA. KARLA IS THE VERY ATTRACTIVE DUTCH/CHINESE GIRL. SHE'S TINY; I MEAN I'M SURE I COULD CLOSE BOTH MY HANDS AROUND HER WAIST. TINY. I'VE BEGUN TO FEEL ALMOST A FATHER FIGURE TO HER THE PAST FEW DAYS. SUCH A SAD THING – SO BEAUTIFUL AND SO INTELLIGENT AND SO SCARED. COCAINE.

AND ROBYN IS LEAVING. SHE'S BEEN SAD ALL EVENING – I DIDINT ASK WHY. BUT I KNOW WHY. ROD, MY ROOMIE HAS BEEN PRETTY MUCH ASLEEP SINCE HE GOT HERE. EVENTUALLY THO I'M SURE I'LL GET TO KNOW HIM

SUNDAY –

UP EARLY – HAD A BATH – OF ALL THINGS. NO MAD RUSH TO THE COFFEE

NOT THIS MORNING EITHER. I WAS THE FIRST ONE AT IT. FINALLY, AFTER JUST A WEEK OF TERRIBLE SLEEP, I WAS GIVEN A PROPER SLEEP MEDICATION THAT ACTUALLY HELPED ME SLEEP - REAL NATURAL SLEEP. WITH NATURAL DREAMS. (ALTHOUGH HIGHLY EROTIC - I MUST BE GETTING BETTER - I HAVEN'T THOUGHT, DREAMT OR PERSUED SEX IN A VERY LONG TIME) BEATS ME WHY I WASN'T OFFERED THIS MEDICATION BEFORE - APPARENTLY IT WAS THERE FOR THE ASKING ALL THIS TIME - FEELING LIKE A LAB RAT HERE SOMETIMES "DESPITE ALL MY RAGE, I AM STILL JUST A RAT IN A CAGE"

AL IS LEAVING THIS MORNING - AND I SEE LAURIE SET HER CLOCK EARLY TO SPEND SOME TIME WITH HIM. NICE. IT'S QUITE PERFECT REALLY. THEY'VE BOTH BEEN COMPLETELY SMITTEN WITH ONE ANOTHER THIS PAST WEEK - BUT BARELY ABLE TO EVEN TOUCH ONE ANOTHER. THE PERFECT COURTSHIP. SOMANCE.

CORRINA - SPEAKING AT HER USUAL ZILLION MILES PER HOUR - IS YAKKIN WITH ROBYN - CAN'T SEEM TO

UNDERSTAND THAT YA JUST GOTTA HAVE A BIT OF FAITH!! AND I DON'T MEAN LIKE "HAVE FAITH IN GOD!!" I JUST MEAN - TRY TO RELAX AND KNOW THAT YOU CAN (AND HAVE TOO) PUT SOME TRUST - AND FAITH - IN PEOPLE AND LIFE. ONE CAN ONLY WORRY AND FRET SO MUCH BEFORE THEY JUST MELT OR EXPLODE. I GUESS COCAINE USE, AND THE LIFESTYLE THAT GOES WITH IT, TRAINS A PERSON TO NOT TRUST - NOT ONE BIT. STUPID FUCKING DRUG.

I'VE OBSERVED THAT PRETTY MUCH EVERYONE LEAVING HERE HAS AMBITIONS TO, BESIDES STAYING CLEAN AND SOBER, START ANEW! REPLACE THEIR CURRENT SITUATION WITH A WHOLE NEW GIG. MYSELF INCLUDED. ONE HAS TO ASK - WHAT CAME FIRST? IS IT AN UNFULFILLING LIFE THAT LEADS TO SUBSTANCE ABUSE? OR DOES SUBSTANCE ABUSE LEAD TO AN UNFULFILLING LIFE? HARD TO SAY FOR SURE - PERSONALLY I BELIEVE IT IS THE FIRST THEORY. I STILL BELIEVE THE BIG PICTURE THEORY - ABOVE AVERAGE INTELLIGENCE AND COUPLED WITH THAT EMOTION DOMINATED PERSONALITY AND NOWHERE TO CHANNEL

ALL OF THAT STUFF. MAN - WHY IS IT SO IMPORTANT TO ME TO GET A HANDLE ON ALL OF THIS? REALLY, IT MAKES NO DIFFERENCE ABOUT THE WHY AND HOW OF IT - IN THE END I'M JUST AN ADDICT, PERIOD.

DON, AKA KENNY ROGERS/MOSES IS STILL HANGING IN THERE - ALTHOUGH IT APPEARS HE'S GOING DOWN HILL. HE WAS BROUGHT IN HERE FOR ATAVAN ADDICTION. SERIOUS SHIT. THE ONES WHO WERE 'PROFESSIONALLY" FUCKED UP ARE THE WORST OFF. - PHARMACEUTICALS ARE VERY WELL DESIGNED, AND LEGAL. (WITH GLOSSY TV ADS)

I'M PRETTY SURE I'LL GET MY "ASSESSMENT INTERVIEW" TODAY, WHICH MEANS I CAN BE OUT OF HERE IN THE NEXT DAY OR TWO. I FEEL I HAVE A MILLION THINGS TO DO - AND YET I STILL DON'T HAVE A PLAN IN PLACE! I GUESS I SHOULD, WHATEVER I DO, INCLUDE TRYING TO FORCE MYSELF TO GET INTO ONE OF THOSE "MEETINGS". I'LL HAVE TROUBLE DOING THAT ON MY OWN - I KNOW THIS - I'M SUCH A CYNIC. BUT I THINK HAVING SOMEONE WITH ME AT LEAST THE FIRST FEW TIMES WOULD BE VERY HELPFUL. WE'LL SEE ABOUT THIS IN, I SUSPECT, THE NEXT DAY OR TWO. MY BRAIN HURTS FROM THINKING SO MUCH.

test.txt — Edited

Seven things that scare me...

1.untimely death (not my own)
2. burning
3.dentists
4.falling
5. nuclear halocaust
6. evil
7. evil that makes sense

Seven things that make me laugh...

1. people
2. people in trouble
3. twisted people
4. nitrous oxide
5. drugs
6. when people make me
7. a few more people

Seven things I love...

1. my child
2. women
3. water
4. sex
5. the wind
6. going fast
7. good use of language

Seven things I loathe...

1. people
2. cruelty
3.dentists
4.stupidity
5.yogurt
6.attitude with no excuse
7. big egos

Seven things I don't understand...

1. women
2. war
3. binary algorythm
4. secrets
5. torture
6. capital punishment
7. americans

test.txt — Edited

Seven things on my desk....

1.cds
2.ashtray
3.dirty cups
4.stains
5. a printer
6. paper paper paper
7. a camera

Seven things I am right now...

1.happy
2.thoughtful
3.alive
4.wishful
5.tired
6.on nicotene
7.curious

Seven somewhat unknown facts about me...

1. i lived before
2. i died before
3. a few tattoos
4. size 12 shoes
5. i pluck grey hair from my chest
6. i do believe in aliens
7. i am a believer

Seven things to do before I die...

1.live
2.explore
3. fiji/tahitii
4.swim with another whale
5. be a grandfather
6.stop nicotene
7. find her

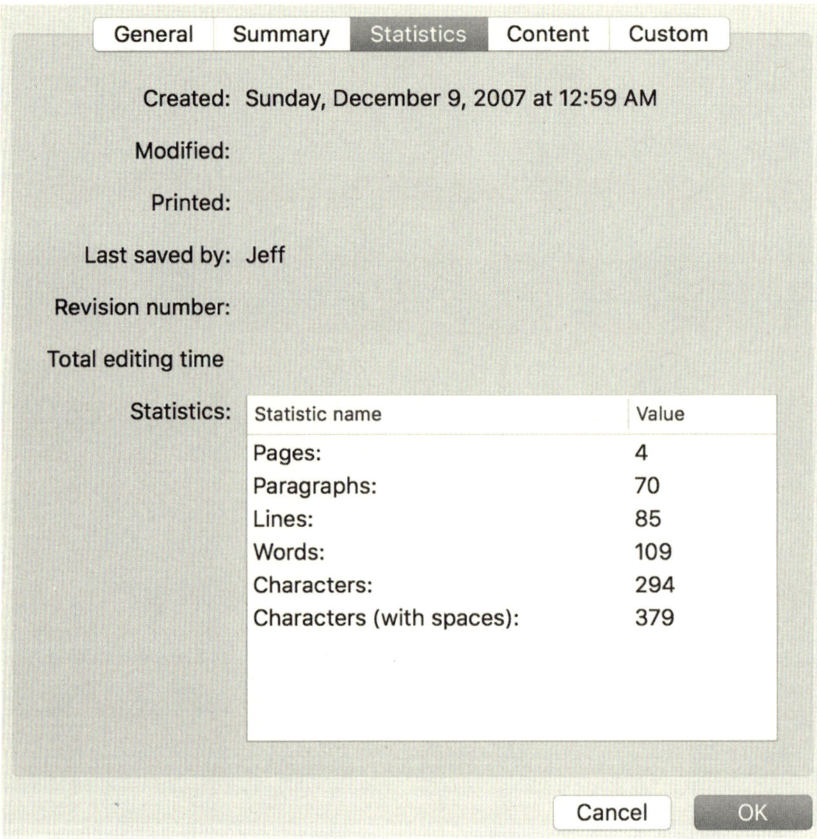
General
Summary
Statistics
Content
Custom
Created: Sunday, December 9, 2007 at 12:59 AM
Modified:
Printed:
Last saved by: Jeff
Revision number:
Total editing time
Statistics:
Statistic name
Value
Pages: 4
Paragraphs: 70
Lines: 85
Words: 109
Characters: 294
Characters (with spaces): 379
Cancel
OK

Andrea Actis

Add a description

Tag Photo · Add Location · Edit

11 · 2 Comments

Like · Comment · Share

Katalin Actis A LOVELY COUPLE... WAITING FOR THE MIRACLE BABY GIRL!:)

Like · Reply · 1

Katalin Actis MARTI"S COMMENT..."THERE WERE 3 IN THIS PICTURE"

Like · Reply · 1

Write a comment...

2007–12–14

Sorry to wake you.

It's okay.

I just . . . I don't understand where he went so fast.

He told me, Sweetie . . . he said he wasn't feeling very well.

On the phone last night?

No, like on Tuesday.

On Tuesday?

I came by when you were out. And he said to me, you know, fuck me, my legs are killing me. From the chair or . . . I don't know. I think he developed maybe a blood clot, you know? It comes very suddenly. I don't know. He's been driving for a couple of weeks so he's been sitting pretty much all through the day too.

The coroner didn't call me back.

She'll call you tomorrow, I'm sure. You left a message, right?

Yeah.

She'll call back tomorrow.

Did the blood-clot theory make sense to her?

The blood-clot theory is a really good theory, Sweetie. He was saying he could barely walk.

When you talked to him last night, did he complain?

Actually he did. He said, you know, I don't know what this is but I can hardly walk . . .

And then he just sat down and died here. Right here on this blanket.

Right here . . . I know. But how amazing, Sweetie? He probably . . . he probably came home . . . his phone was in his pocket . . . raincoat was here . . . the phone card was there. So he probably put down the phone card and then he . . . you know, he kind of . . . he probably felt something. And then went holy fuck. Just turned around and . . . I don't know.

I wish I could have been there. To comfort him.

I know, Sweetie. I feel that too. But on the one hand . . . I know him. I know him, you know? When this is happening, I think . . . you probably *know* this isn't good as it's happening. In his mind he probably went shit, I'm so glad Andrea's not here.

God . . . I'm going to miss him so much.

As long as we live we're going to miss him, Sweetie. And that's just something, you know . . . that's just how it will be. Fucking hell, Jeff.

I can't believe this.

I can't either.

I can't believe this. What the fuck is going on?

I don't know, Sweetie ... but, you know, basically everything that's happened so far, like yesterday, today ... he's probably smiling because it's just been absolutely perfect the way things have been.

People have been so good.

That teacher of yours, my god. That lasagna. It's just so ... I just don't think ... I mean you sometimes *say* I fucking wish I was dead, you know? He wanted to finish it off. Fucking October was a horrible month. I don't know how ...

I'm so glad he got a bit better, though, before he died.

Well this is it, you know. Deep inside ... he hoped things were going to get better. But deep inside he knew. He was scared, you know. For him to take himself to the friggin' hospital last month, you know how bad it must have been. So I think the doctor told him, listen buddy, things don't look very good. So you better take it easy.

I can't believe he was lying here dead when I came home. He was just lying here ...

I've seen him looking like that so many times, quite frankly, in the last little while. Looking, you know, dead. And I would pick him up. I would shake him. I would swear at him—*Motherfucker*, you know?

Yeah, I've seen him in strange positions. Face down. But here he was totally sunken. And his hand looked really weird and stiff and I touched it and it was really cold. And I went *Dad, Dad, Daddy* . . .

Oh, Sweetie. Did you scream or no?

No, I just frantically looked for my phone and couldn't find it. The neighbour called 9-1-1.

Were they here fast?

No idea. Under ten minutes, I think. Oh god . . . my dad! What was he thinking when it happened? Like what exactly was he thinking and hoping for?

Oh, Sweetheart.

I need him.

I know. I need him too, believe it or not. I can't believe I won't be able to share anything good or bad with him anymore. I mean, things that will happen to you. Good things, you know. It'll be really nice, but to be able to share it with him . . .

Oh my god . . . I just want him to not be dead!

I know, Sweetie. It's not going to be easy for us. But I also know he would so be upset if he knew how upset we are.

He would fucking understand.

Well, yeah . . . he would understand, of course.

I just hope he makes himself felt and present in obvious ways—

—he will—

—I mean I don't want to have to wonder if he's present. He has to be. Please, Dad, make it obvious that you're still with me in this stupid apartment.

He will. He will always be here. You guys had such a special bond. Even after you called him an ignorant prick, you know, before you went to Ontario. When David was dying. But you guys had such a connection that I can't, I just can't believe that . . . I mean my grandma Elizabeth, she's been dead I don't know how many years. And still when I have something that's tremendously difficult, that's when I turn to her, like what the fuck? She makes me feel like Jeff is okay now.

Do you just hear her voice or do you see her?

I kind of see her. But it's more like a warm feeling that I get.

How often does she come?

It's like a radiant feel.

How often does that happen?

Whenever I'm in trouble, she's always there. No exceptions. Now it's going to be Jeff too.

She's told you Dad's okay?

Absolutely.

What did she say?

> I got so upset today on the toilet and just went *AARGHGJLLFH*! And she reassured me everything is okay . . .

Did you actually hear her voice?

> No, Sweetie, I don't hear her voice. But it's *almost* her voice. This big positive weight that I feel. I'm not sure how to explain it. But it gave me a total feeling and confidence that he is okay. I mean I'm sure he's going holy fuck, did I really die? Like I wanted to, you know, but not really! Not quite yet. But he'll always be here, Sweetie. Believe that. And I'll do my best at cooking a few things that he taught me how to cook. Swiss Steak and . . . you know . . .

I'm just scared he's gonna ignore me because he won't want to creep me out. Or worry me. So I get over it more quickly or something. But I want it to be really obvious . . . I want my house to be fucking haunted.

> I know, Sweetie. But I also think that everything you do, you'll also kind of mentally discuss with him, you know. You'll kind of . . . like what I do with my grandma. And it's all good. It's not, you know, freaky. It's like a conversation that is more or less just warm reassurance. Because we *know* what to do. It's just that extra push—like this is *exactly* what you gotta do.

He's dead, Mom. He's in a freezer. Cut up. He was right here yesterday. We watched that fucked-up autopsy video on YouTube together last week . . . sharing a big salad bowl of Kraft Dinner because we were both too tired to wash the small bowls. We were laughing so hard.

> I know. That's kind of what's scaring me. Not scaring me—I know it's natural, he's not feeling anything. But the thing is that we have to sort of make some arrangements soon for someone

to come and, you know, take him wherever. I don't want to be there for the cremation. I just want to leave it this way. I don't want to be at the cremation, I just want . . . I don't fucking know . . .

I know I *don't* want to sit in the same room as the oven or something. Actually I have no idea. I don't know what the options are. What are the options?

I think we have to phone around and, you know, find stuff out.

There's a place right on Hastings there. I mean . . . I wouldn't mind seeing him again if I knew he wasn't, like, decomposing or anything.

You know, Sweetie, lying face up . . . he wasn't looking like Jeff. You didn't look, did you?

No.

Good, Sweetie. He was swollen, his nose was kinda smushed.

Yeah, I'm so glad I didn't come in the room again. I don't need to see him again. Were his eyes open?

No, Sweetie, his eyes weren't open.

I'm so glad he was just on his face or whatever. He knows how much I hate dead bodies with their eyes open . . . how that corpse in *Kindergarten Cop* fucked me up for life . . .

His eyes weren't open, Sweetie. Well . . . okay. I guess maybe they were a tiny bit open, but not really . . . not really open.

Oh my god. He's dead!

He's really dead. I know. I can't fucking believe it.

He's just . . . dead . . .

I know. I *know* . . . and I *see*, I just can't accept. And you know what, Sweetie? The only thing is time . . . yeah, Jeff is no more. But at the same time I think he will be here and he will want us to keep going . . . keep doing what we're doing. And for you there are certain things. We talked a lot . . .

Your last conversation? Just tell me now.

You're not ready, Andrea. It was forty minutes. When you're ready I'll tell you.

Jesus Christ . . . fine. Should we eat the last of these gummy worms?

Yeah, I think we should. I brought these over for us on Tuesday . . . he needed insoles from Shoppers. Fuck, Jeff, I've known you since I was twenty years old.

It's just so weird that Jady would call me last night, right around the time it happened . . .

Sweetie, you're sensitive enough to tap into these things. And Jeff was sensitive too. But I don't think he knew he was dying last night. He was saying how he just got paid and wanted to make us a nice Swiss Steak. We were gonna go to Superstore tomorrow. But again we mostly talked about you. He said when he's feeling better he's gonna get onto you about your whole egg-donation thing. You know, he is so old-fashioned in a way . . . he was so, you know . . . that whole new concept of this. But his explanation in a way made sense to me. I know her, he says . . . I know that if she goes off and she's in her fourth year

> of school and Krista calls her and says oh, you should see how lovely the kid is and he or she did this or that, you'd have a hard time not being there and sharing this. And I said Jeff, I don't know. I don't know what to say.

I told her recently that Dad wasn't comfortable with it . . .

> I mean, he said to me, when we went to Bon's . . . he said he had a bad feeling. I said fuck Jeff, I don't know how to deal with this. I don't know enough about this whole sort of subject to really know how I feel about this. Like, what I know is that Andrea has been through a whole bunch of counselling and it's being done properly. And he says oh, she's just trying to fulfill someone's else's dream and I said yeah, that's kind of true.

I'm actually trying to fulfill my own dream. I can't think of anything more interesting . . .

> Andrea, this is her dream. She approached *you*. You would've never ever conceived of this. She approached you with this whole concept.

So?

> I'm just saying it was her dream, it wasn't your thing. You were just going merrily along being a student and learning stuff until Krista approached you and said well, what about this? And you were tickled and touched by the thought that she actually thinks of you to be that person who will make this happen. I mean that's a big thing.

When I talked with Dad very recently about this, he still couldn't give me a clear answer for why it's a bad thing.

Because it's an emotional thing, Sweetie, and he knew deep inside that it's . . . he knows you. He knows how you are when you see puppies.

Well yeah, then I'm gonna see this child and feel related to it and love it and that'll be fine.

It *will* be fine, but it also . . . once that child is there things can happen in the sense that—

—you're only saying this because—

—I'm saying what he's saying—

—well exactly! And he's dead now, so you can have your own opinion about it.

I'm half-and-half, Sweetie. I haven't tipped either way. That's how I'll be. What I feel is that you should have your own child with someone you love first. See, we were still going to have this big discussion while you were away, you know? He wanted to be a grandfather. I don't think he would've changed his mind but I kind of wanted to persuade him that if you said yes, it's for a good reason, like trust her with her judgments Jeff!

He's trusted me with everything else.

Yeah, and this was something else. This was different.

Yeah. And so is this.

I'm just gonna miss him. I'm just gonna fucking miss him. Damn.

Here's his stupid hat. Wait, what about this cash? I gave you fifty, right?

Yeah . . . so you should have $350 there.

Weird, hang on a sec . . . I did give you fifty, right? So sixty, seventy . . . how did he spend almost $300 last night?

I don't know, Sweetie. Unless he had money in his jeans pocket and it fell out or something? I don't know what he does with fucking money.

Where are his jeans?

On him!

Do they give those back to us?

I hope so . . .

I just can't believe he died.

I can't believe it either, Sweetie. I'm praying I'll wake up and this is just not happening. But I also . . . I feel it's somehow very true that this is happening.

Where the hell did he go? And his money? Maybe it's in the Pony.

Was I the last call on his phone?

Yeah.

Oh god . . . oh Jeffrey. We love you, Jeffrey. I have to fucking pee . . .

Elastoplast
PANSEMENT EN RUBAN
Permatex
FAST ORANGE
Hand Cleaner
ORIGINAL
PONCE
STIM-U-DENT
ST-RÉMY
AUTHENTIC
VSOP
NOKIA

Seven somewhat unknown fac... me
1. i lived before
2. i died before
3. a few tattoos
4. size 12 shoes
5. i pluck g...
6. i do beli...
7. i am a believ...
JEFFREY BENVENUTO ACTIS
September 6, 1954 - December 14, 2007

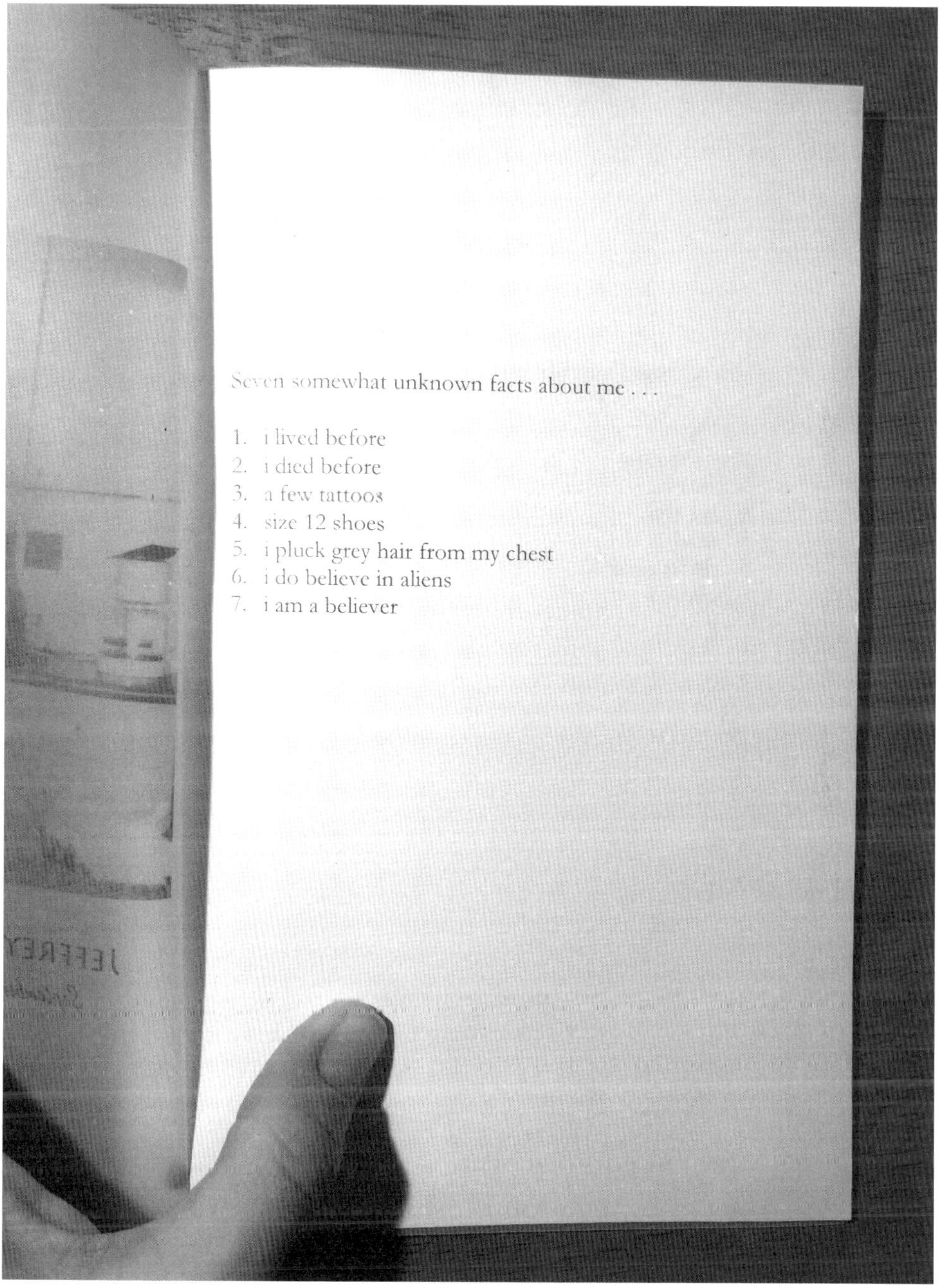
Seven somewhat unknown facts about me . . .
1. i lived before
2. i died before
3. a few tattoos
4. size 12 shoes
5. i pluck grey hair from my chest
6. i do believe in aliens
7. i am a believer

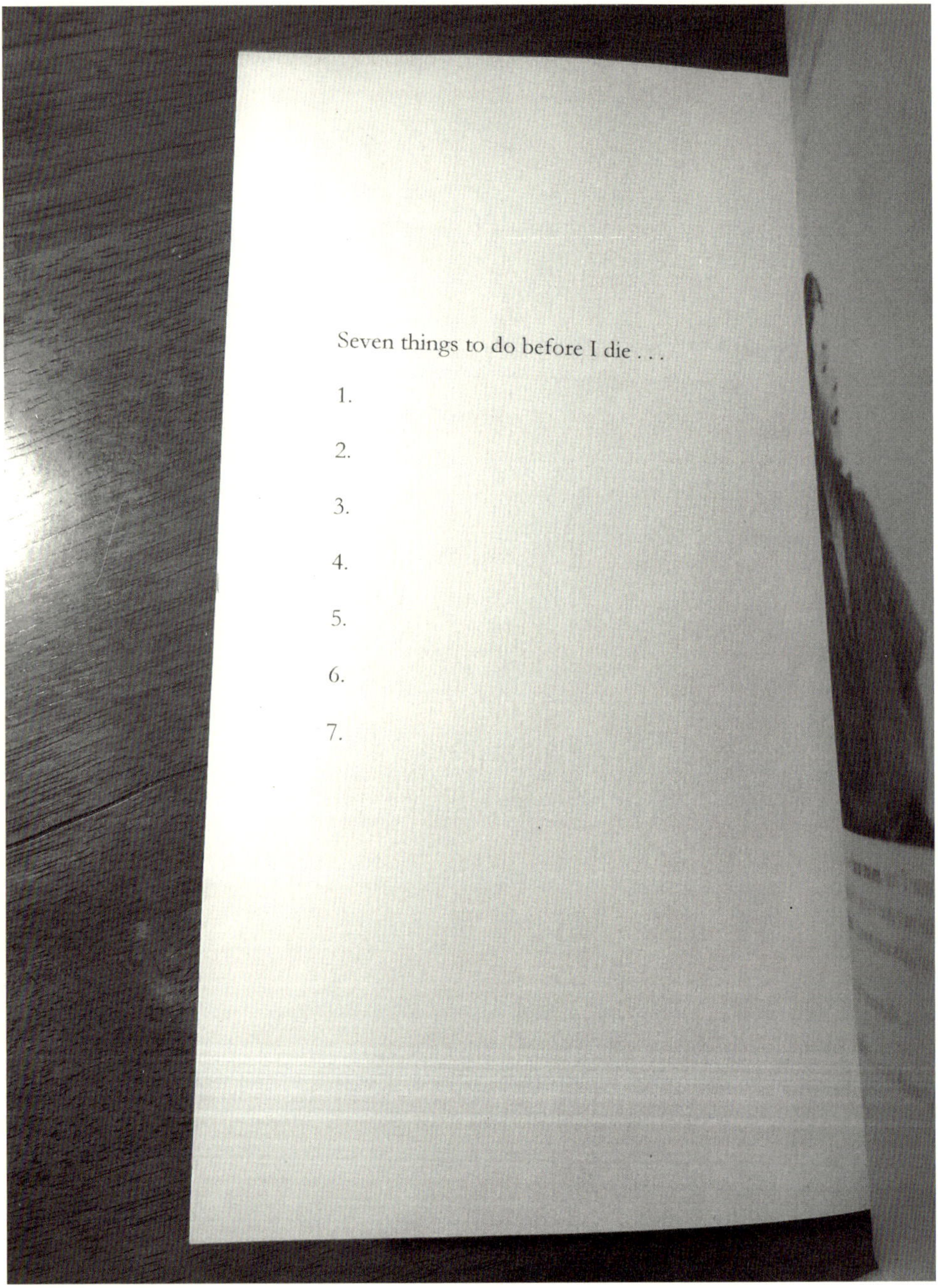
Seven things to do before I die . . .
1.
2.
3.
4.
5.
6.
7.

"To recover, after each blow, the original balance of life and death, to sacrifice to one as to the other, to one after the other, to be dead with death and living with life up to your last sigh (which is not death's triumph, but forsaking the body): this is health."

—Edmond Jabès, *The Book of Questions*

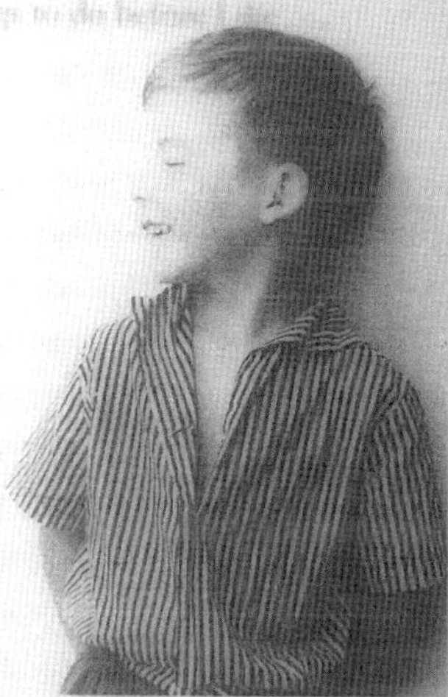

"In the course of time I was more and more conscious, too, that this affliction was not due to any defects of nature but rather to a profusion of gifts and powers which had not attained to harmony."

—Hermann Hesse, *Steppenwolf*

"I always have been blessed with an uncowling sense of train..."

—Jeffrey-Dad

phone home

Andrea Actis <missactis@gmail.com>
to Dad

Thu, Jan 3, 2008, 4:48 AM

3 Attachments

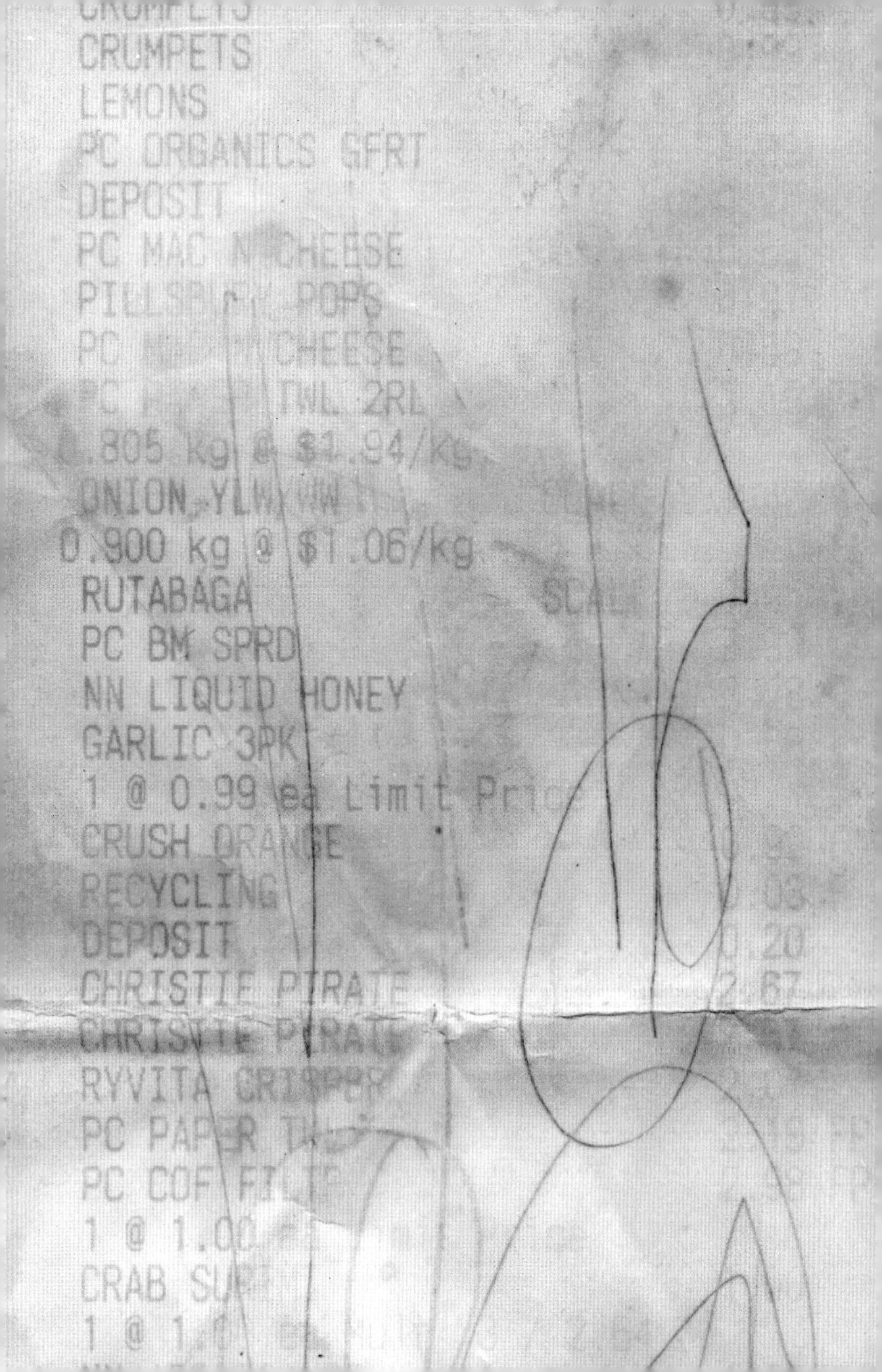
CRUMPETS
LEMONS
PC ORGANICS GFRT
DEPOSIT
PC MAC N CHEESE
PC [illegible] CHEESE
PC [illegible] TWL 2RL
.805 kg @ $1.94/kg
ONION YLW [illegible]
0.900 kg @ $1.06/kg
RUTABAGA SCA[illegible]
PC BM SPRD
NN LIQUID HONEY
GARLIC 3PK
1 @ 0.99 ea Limit Pric[illegible]
CRUSH ORANGE
RECYCLING [illegible]0.08
DEPOSIT 0.20
CHRISTIE PIRATE 2.67
CHRISTIE PIRATE
RYVITA CRI[illegible]
PC PAPER T[illegible]
PC COF F[illegible]
1 @ 1.0[illegible]
CRAB SU[illegible]
1 @ 1[illegible]

I AM STILL BLOWN AWAY BY THE VOLUME OF PEOPLE ARRIVING AND LEAVING HERE

Does no one notice this? The ladies and gentlemen who should be walking on the pavement are floating.

THE DAYS HERE ARE STRUCTURED AROUND MEALS AND SNACKS, WITH A FEW MEDS AND SESSIONS TOSSED IN.

They poured me some lemonade and a girl with red lips held my glass while I drank. The hostess offered me a meringue on a silver salver and a girl in a pure white dress put the meringue in my mouth.

I GAVE OMAR A SAMOSA LAST NIGHT - HE LIT UP LIKE A TREE.

Since everyone was treating me so well I was a little surprised that they were so unanimous in holding me back when I tried to return to the piano.

MAYBE ANOTHER TIME. IN MY NEXT LIFE PERHAPS?

I realized that whether I allowed myself to be stabbed or ran away, my end had come.

I PREFER TO SLIP AWAY QUIETLY.

And now everything was seized by speed and fell into the distance.

PRETTY MUCH EVERYONE - EVERYONE - HAS BEEN HERE BEFORE - AND WILL RETURN.

And it is fortunate that tomorrow will be a day on which, unlikely as it may seem, one will be able to see everything.

I SUSPECT TODAY I WILL SPEAK WITH SOMEONE ABOUT LEAVING HERE.

Tell me everything, from beginning to end.

UP EARLY - HAD A BATH - OF ALL THINGS.

A way of life so natural that it borders on the excessive!

JUST ANOTHER DAY IN LIMBO.

I wandered on for a while with closed eyes, keeping myself awake only by a loud and regular clapping of my hands.

I WISH I HAD ARRIVED FEELING WORSE.

Just wait, something's going to happen today. And it did, too.

ONE CAN ONLY WORRY AND FRET SO MUCH BEFORE THEY JUST MELT OR EXPLODE.

I could not bear the strain of seeing around me the things of the earth.

THIS WOULD BE A GOOD TIME TO SPEAK WITH SOMEONE, BUT I BELIEVE I HAVE TO WAIT A BIT LONGER FOR THAT.

You've never had so discreet a listener as I.

THE ATMOSPHERE HAS CHANGED DRAMATICALLY IN ONE DAY.

I understand a dead man was carried in here just now. Would you be kind enough to let me see him?

I REMEMBER BEING SO COMPELLED WONDERING HOW FAR IT CAN GO.— IS THERE A LIMIT TO SMALL?

I don't understand it. But I don't even know if there is a connection.

I KNOW THE RIGHT WORDS ARE IN THERE BUT THEY GENERALLY ELUDE ME.

One will have to struggle here as anywhere else, but at least one won't have to do it with graceful movements.

I GUESS WHAT I'M GETTING AT HERE IS— MY LIFE HAS BECOME QUITE UNNEEDED— TO MYSELF AND ALL THOSE AROUND ME.

I have done nobody any harm, nobody has done me any harm, but nobody will help me.

I GET A HEADACHE AND FEEL LIKE I'VE BEEN THROUGH A FUCKING FREDDY KRUGER MOVIE.

But for me there was now a third possibility of perishing.

"DESPITE ALL MY RAGE- I AM STILL JUST A RAT IN A CAGE"

It was a long time since I'd seen it like this; I was moved and reminded of certain days when I thought I had seen it in the same way.

ITS HARD TO THINK WITH A (RELATIVELY) CLEAR MIND.

Over the deserted, evenly lit street stood a large moon in a slightly clouded, and therefore unusually extended, sky. On the frozen snow one had to take short steps.

IT'S THE WEEKEND - NOT THAT IT MEANS ANYTHING IN PARTICULAR HERE. JUST THOUGHT I'D MENTION THAT.

Why has everything become so quiet?

I MADE A PROMISE I WOULDN'T GO BACK TO REVIEW THESE PAGES - AT LEAST WHILE I'M STILL HERE.

"I wasn't in need of your information," I said, which happened to be true.

SOME PEOPLE GOT THEIR REAL NAMES, SOME GOT ALIASES.

It worked and we came fast enough into the interior of a vast but as yet unfinished landscape.

I HAVE A BURNING DESIRE TO LEAVE HERE TODAY.

Heard someone sob softly from afar.

BEDTIME.

I let a strong wind blow against us in long gusts.

I STILL HAVE SO MANY PAGES TO FILL.

Then I closed my eyes so as to shut out the bad light.

IN THE END - TURNS OUT HE WAS SPEAKING ABOUT HIMSELF (I KNEW THIS)

And I'm grateful.

TESTING TESTING

Testing. Testing testing. Testing.

How's this?

Hey, Dad.

So the date is December 14th, 2008. It's, uh, Sunday night. I'm in my relatively new home in Providence, Rhode Island, doing my . . . well just about completing my first semester of a five-year PhD program in English and I'm surrounded by books and notes and once again I'm getting away with writing on Simone de Beauvoir and *The Ethics of Ambiguity* and failure somehow.

Um, I'm gonna try to talk to the camera like it's you. You bought me this thing with Mom before I went to Panama, two Januaries ago I guess. I don't use the camera as much as I should but I figured this would be a good opportunity. There's that video you took of me when I was getting packed to go on that trip and I recently found the video and there's like a really sad Sigur Rós song playing in the background and I remember that night so clearly . . . hanging out in the bedroom you'd eventually die in. Oh god, then all the black mould that developed when Tiz and Julian moved in . . . anyway. So it's kind of like, yeah, it's like this is your . . . I'm now pretending this is you.

Um . . . these are your ashes! In the container you used to keep your weed in. I think you got this thing at a garage sale in Rexdale when I was little . . . where that guy tried to sell you his bookcase by pretending it was made of actual dinosaur bones or whatever. Anyway, yeah . . . it took a while to figure out exactly what to do with your ashes but I knew we'd have to listen to this Brian Eno song while doing something with them at some point. You always said you wanted it at your funeral or whatever . . . Brian Eno and good olives and . . . well, lots of booze. So yeah.

This is just a little candle from home that I've been lighting every so often. I lit it when I first moved in here and then I lit it on your birthday and then I lit it when I had my conversation with the medium from Lily Dale. And, yeah, I'm lighting it now.

So I figure I'll just, like . . . as I've told my new therapist, I've really felt like I need to write down sort of absolutely everything I remember, everything I remember happening. Wait, is this thing even on? Just a sec.

Okay.

So I just couldn't get around to writing down any of the details this past year—*Dad details*, as I've been identifying the task on my to-do lists. But you know my relationship to writing, it's more than a little complicated. So my therapist suggested I videotape myself or record myself somehow and this seemed like a good way to do it. Anyway.

Uh, in case you can't tell, I'm also burning some nag champa as I talk to you here. My roommate just left to go home for the holidays and she hates incense. But once she leaves it's okay, I guess, to burn it.

Um . . . okay. So it's been exactly a year since you died. And I really,

really hate that you died. This has been the worst year ever for me, as I'm sure you've been able to *observe*. Like I was messed up to begin with, then this! I was so fucking angry at you but loved you so, so much. Still do. And anyway . . . I guess I don't exactly know where to start.

There've been things popping to mind, just little things that I've wanted to remember, like how you'd say *Som-a-nice! Som-a-nice!* when something pleased you and you wanted to caricature your own, you know, Italianness. I really miss that . . . the rare, unfortunately, feeling of getting to know with certainty that you were pleased with something . . . in a good mood for whatever mysterious reason. I've thought of us driving from Toronto to Edmonton right before Grade Eight was supposed to start and the stupid *butt-turd-toast* joke we kept making that almost killed us. *Butt-turd-toast!* We were so sleep-deprived and constipated . . . I guess it didn't really matter that we had no idea what we were doing driving to Edmonton really . . . it was still so much fun. And there've been so many things like that, little things you'd do or say that briefly indicated to me an okayness with you. Looking through photos I'm taken back to, you know . . . moments that were impossibly hard. But I do, you know, really miss you picking me up from SFU and cooking me cheeseburgers and stew and those parsley dumplings you were making like every day towards the end for some reason.

I guess I just miss caring for you, Dad. I worried so much about you in recent times . . . we all did and I know you had a hard time, you know, doing that to us or whatever. You felt so guilty. If you don't already know, I made that one erasure poem-thing with a few parts of your journal and that Kafka story recently . . . I hope that's okay. I had a hard time doing it and was so nervous about how it'd turn out . . . whether it'd feel political enough or whatever

So, uh, anyway, I guess I just want to recount as much as I possibly can, you know, from the day before you died, up till sort of the memorial and then the . . . you know . . . when we went to scatter your ashes. Though that weekend on the island is pretty well documented. Reba took a million pictures, including, like, close-ups of your bone fragments washing down the stream. Totally weird but I'm really really grateful she did that.

So it was . . . ah, sorry! I just so often think about the day you picked me up from writing my stupid GRE and the smell of that lotion, that kind of expensive lotion I couldn't really afford but that I'd bought two bottles of anyway just in case it ended up being spontaneously discontinued or something. And how you picked me up from the mall out in Burnaby where I wrote my exam and it was just like . . . I don't know, for some reason I think of that afternoon a lot and how sort of strangely positive you were. And you'd just met with . . . what the fuck's his name—the guy you were gonna start working for soon. See I'm already forgetting stuff. Dale? No, not Dale. It'll come to mind. The guy at Horizon, anyway. Your new boss who was really nice and who wanted to make you a manager or something. You were all, you know, understandably intimidated by the prospect of having to do a job you had no idea how to do but at least there were no toxic fumes. But, I dunno, you picked me up in the Pony and it was just, like, nice as hell. Like I felt I'd done fairly well on at least one part of the test so bought myself a new M·A·C concealer and some lip balm and perfume. You picked me up and we drove to X-Site and had the souvlaki lunch special. And it was just . . . for whatever reason, that day sticks out. And, you know, maybe some other time . . . I dunno . . . maybe it'll be important to recount all the nightmarish shit that led to you needing to move in with me a month and a half before you dropped dead. How all the rich people you worked for would never pay you for the work you did on their yachts . . . how your mom took everything from us when I was a kid . . . how you never got the treatment and support you needed . . . how your rage did nothing but work to destroy you . . . how resigned I always felt to you, you know, commiting suicide . . . anyway. It was really bad. Right now I mostly remember and want to remember what was wonderful. Our laughing fits. Our psychic connection. I know I over-identify with you probably, but fuck it . . . I'm hanging on for now.

So you moved in at the beginning of November. And you just . . . you worked on your computer a lot and you'd make us really good dinners . . . fish and chips and Swiss Steak and vegetable soup . . . you know, cheeseburgers and stew . . . whatever. Totally delicious. And you fixed the hole in the wall . . . the hole I'd made when I threw a mug at Jady's head after he cheated on me the year before. And, yeah, I was completely happy to have you around because you're my favourite person in the world and I felt like I was doing something to help. You didn't have to be homeless or whatever and you could also drive me to school or work or whatever.

So, December 13th, Thursday morning . . . I was up probably around 5:30. You were already awake. You were in your room, and I'd woken up to put the finishing touches on my applications, put them in envelopes and address them and whatnot. And then you came into the kitchen and we had a cup of coffee together. And you . . . sorry, just before I forget, I really miss going to Superstore with you! How things were always like bought-out on Sunday evenings when for whatever fucking reason we always decided we needed to go to Superstore. It's Sunday night again, great, let's go to Superstore even though there's not gonna be any food left! Anyway, I really miss that and still have kind of a hard time walking through grocery stores.

Okay. So the morning of the 13th we're talking and I'm really excited. I'm proud of my applications and talking to you sort of about what my plan is, and I'm telling you about David Harvey, I guess. The

Spaces of Hope book. And I told you you needed to read it and you said you would. And . . . yeah, just sort of fantasizing about getting a SSHRC grant and saying I could help you and, you know, you could drive me to wherever I was gonna end up for grad school. And I was just, yeah, super excited and you were excited for me too, in a good mood. Pretty calm, you know? And you said that out of all the places I might end up, Providence would be the likeliest to get you on a plane.

What else did we talk about? That's all I really remember, unfortunately . . . I guess I must've been worried about the paper I still hadn't finished for my Feminisms class . . . but we had a really nice talk for like a couple of hours, actually. And then you had to go to work. And I, uh . . . I took my applications to the Shoppers downtown, to the post office, then I went to the dentist and got some redundant kind of, like, treatment on one of my back molars. Like he shaved it down a little so I wouldn't put so much pressure on this one particular spot. I have no idea, but it cost $90 and seemed like a total waste of money. Then I guess on the way home I talked for way too long to that evangelist guy at the bus stop. I was listening to *In Rainbows* on repeat all day. Then what happened . . . ?

Fuck, sorry, this tea's really good. It's called "Unity." Tastes like a Christmas tree. You'd probably say you hate it and I would try to convince you that you don't hate it.

Okay . . . so then you came home from work, I guess . . . oh! Garth! Garth was your boss's name. Garth gave you a Christmas card with, like, some kind of actually good joke in it. And a gift card to The Keg. And you were just really sort of touched and positive about your new job and you'd gotten a paycheque and, uh, I guess you wanted to make dinner for me that night but I sort of had plans to go to Mike Barnholden's book launch. So, you know, I was upset about my latest breakup probably . . . yeah, for sure I was. And you were trying to, you know, tell me it was going to be okay. Then we drove to my bank . . . it was raining so fucking hard, so we drove there . . . and I realized I'd forgotten my wallet so I couldn't actually deposit your cheque. And for some reason you were, like, totally okay with it, you know? Like okay, we just have to go back, that's fine! It's normal! Which was sort of surprising to me in that moment. Then in the meantime, like . . . this is what probably gave you the fucking heart attack . . . but the window of the Pony kept falling down and we had no means of keeping it up. The car was getting totally soaked. So when we went back for my wallet I also grabbed all those erasers, like fifteen Pink Pearl erasers I'd bought for you to put under your laptop to keep it from, you know, overheating. But nothing would keep that fucking window up. We deposited your cheque, anyway . . . then you drove me over to Main Street . . . and I think we took King Edward. I remember you pointed out the 7-Eleven at 25th and Fraser or something and told me how earlier in the week you'd sat on that very curb eating a bunch of donuts in the middle of the afternoon. It was really funny . . . we both laughed so hard at how impossible it seemed for you to adequately explain or do justice to how good the donuts were or something. Then we turned onto Main and I got out outside of Montmartre and said I'd call you if I needed a ride later or if I was going to be, you know, too-too late. Which, as you know, I didn't do. And I'm pretty sure I said *I love you* and you said *I love you too*, you know . . . *I'll see you later tonight*. And that was the last thing we said to each other. Which was a pretty good thing to say, I suppose. We were pretty lucky.

You weren't happy about me donating eggs at that point, for various reasons, some of which I'm still convinced were paranoid or exaggerated or whatever. You can see that I was right, right? That I'm not wanting to go snatch Krista's new baby from her, right? But that was what you talked about with Mom on the phone before you ran out of your phone card and had to go down to the Shell. Then I guess when you ... you were trying to get her to come over to watch *The Astronaut Farmer*. You'd been downloading a lot movies recently and really liked that one ... I just hadn't had time to sit down and watch it with you. Though I did have time to watch that twenty-minute autopsy video with you a week or two before you had your own autopsy! Pretty awful. I had a hard time dealing with *that*, I must say ...

You know, I don't know, I'm actually feeling okay. I like talking like this. I mean yeah, I'm on antidepressants, that's why I'm not sobbing or screaming into my pillow or running naked into the snow. But anyway ...

So you paused the movie ... Mom wasn't gonna come over but she was happy to talk on the phone with you. And I guess you were drinking, you had a mickey of your brandy, though you hadn't been drinking at all since moving in with us. And I guess at some point that night you'd found or bought some clothespins and snapped them in half to try keep the window of the Pony up. I imagine they're still wedged in there, holding the window up, you know ... the Pony's back at Marti and Tata's now and I bet the stupid fucking clothespins are still doing their thing. So, yeah, you paused the movie, told Mom you'd call her back, walked to the gas station—seems you bought two coffees, maybe one for you and one for me, or one for Mom in case she changed her mind and came over to hang out, or two for you ... I have no idea what you were thinking buying two large coffees at 2am or whenever. And then you came home and went back upstairs ... your legs had been really hurting ... but maybe you took the stairs anyway? And then, you know, I don't really know what happened to you. But yeah ... I have no idea what happened to you.

You had a heart attack and I don't know ... your coat was still on, or maybe your coat was off. I think your keys and cellphone were sort of right by your hand on the bed.

So I'd been out at that book launch earlier in the evening and then Reg and I went to Hoko's. And there was a launch for *The Liar* and it was a really fun night actually. Kind of weird . . . I was drunk and exhausted . . . but there was that really pretty UBC student who ended up karaokeing to that Fleetwood Mac song that will forever remind me of the night you died. Then Hoko's closed and Reg drove me home. We sat in his car for about an hour just silently listening to that soul CD . . . I'll put one of the tracks on now, actually . . .

So we listened to this whole CD in his car and then said goodnight. And I was thinking I was so excited to announce to you that I'd been sitting in a car right downstairs for over an hour listening to this amazing mix CD with this nice person. And I got upstairs and couldn't find my keys . . . I was using that stupid brown bag with all the stitching coming apart at the bottom so everything kind of disappears in there. Eventually, you know, I find my keys, and I go into the apartment. Your bedroom door's open and the lights are on. And I walk into the room and you're face down on the bed. Totally, totally face down . . . like *so* face down . . . it looked so fucked up, Dad. And I kind of, for a second, I thought you were just passed out. Then I shook you and pleaded with you for a minute to wake up. But I totally knew. I knew this was the worst possible thing that could be happening.

So this is like 3:30 in the morning and I go bang on the neighbour's door. I'm going *My dad's dead, my dad's dead!* and she's like *Are you sure?* and I'm like *Yeah, I'm fucking sure*. So she called 9-1-1. And I went in the living room and phoned Mom and Marti and Tata . . . and, uh, they didn't answer at first and then Marti called back. I said I needed to talk to Mom so she put her on and I just screamed *Dad's dead, Dad's dead!* Mom told me later that she'd thought I was completely strung out on drugs. Then the cops came . . . there was that woman cop with the short brown hair who was not, like, the friendliest. She just came into the living room and towering over me with crossed arms was like, *Well, your father* HAS *passed away* . . . then Mom and Marti and Tata arrived a little later, I guess. I remember seeing them come down the hallway looking so scared and shaky and upset. And then, god, I have no idea. There were those two paramedics who came and they were much nicer . . . one kind of had tears in his eyes . . .

Sorry, I'm gonna change the music again. How about *Dark Side of the Moon*? We always said . . . for some reason I always told myself that if I listened to this after you died, it would always remind me of you. I knew it would work like that, you know?

Okay. It's insanely chilly in here actually. Just a sec.

So yeah . . . they turned you over. They turned your body over and Mom and Marti and Tata—no, before they turned it over I went in there and said *I love you so much* and *Please stay with me, please stay here, please cause poltergeists in my stupid apartment* . . . things like that. I didn't spend too much time with you. Then I went back to the living room and they turned you over and, yeah, everyone took turns saying goodbye. Mom assures me that it's better I didn't see you like that, looking all weird. I'm sure you realize how grateful I am that I didn't have to see your face at all. Then they put you on a gurney and covered you in a white bag or a black bag . . . I don't know, I couldn't watch. I'd seen them do that to David's body the year before and I was just in shock at this point, I couldn't move from the living room. The coroner was there and she was friendly . . . I kept thinking you would really like her. She was Australian or something.

And then . . . you were just gone. You were completely gone. And that was the beginning of the worst year of my life. Yeah . . . you know . . . you *must know* . . . I'd had those ten seconds of complete fucking euphoria, like utter liberation from you after the cop lady told me you were definitely dead and I ran into the other bedroom . . . just sort of stared into the closet full of shit, looking for something to smash then kind of realizing I didn't want to do that. Even that morning, talking to you about my applications, I had no fucking idea how I was ever going to be able to leave you . . .

Then we all just kind of sat around for a while, and then I slept a couple of hours, maybe. In the morning I called a bunch of people . . . I had this intense urge to phone as many people as I could and tell them what'd happened. I had to hear myself say it as many times as possible. I probably called like forty people.

Where did you go? I kept asking. *Where the fuck did you go?*

Then of course we took me to the doctor and I got some Ativan and some other kind of sleeping pill. Took a couple of those a day for a while. We didn't really touch your room. We ate the gummy worms and got some Pirate cookies and put an unopened Pom Pom on your pillow. Then what? I don't know. Then Steve came over with the lasagna and gave me a card . . . basically the kindest and wisest letter anyone's ever written to me . . .

And I was able to talk to you pretty well, actually. I only did it a few times but I'd lie on your bed and just talk to you like we were on the phone or something. Like ET-phone-home or something. Then it stopped seeming possible to do that, somehow. I don't know why.

Ivan and Stacey were incredibly wonderful during this period, too. Ivan reserved the Sk'ıwıtsut Hut at Lighthouse Park for your memorial . . . we ordered enough trays of Stepho's souvlaki to feed half the city . . . then there was the guy from A Basic Cremation who came and talked to us. Same guy who cremated Mimi, actually. And we wrote you letters on that, like, arbitrary rhinoceros stationery . . . I can't really remember what I said in mine . . . but everyone wrote you one. And I think I put that photo of me eating my first-ever cheeseburger on Sauble Beach . . . fuck I should've kept better track of what I had them cremate with you. That bamboo cross, I think, that Mimi gave me and that I'd always take on planes with me so that I'd be, you know, blessed or whatever if my plane were to explode. I gave the cremation guy the cross and my rhinoceros note and the cheeseburger photo . . . actually you always thought it was Wasaga Beach . . . I don't know . . .

The other memory I keep having is from way back . . . when Steve Chattergoon caught that water snake when I was a kid. It's so weird how often I think of that, of how absolutely scandalized I felt to learn that snakes were a thing you could pull out of a lake. Then going ice fishing with you guys that one time . . . I sometimes think of that and can hardly believe I'm a person who's ever once gone ice fishing. I remember you let me drive Val's minivan across the ice . . . my first time ever behind the wheel, I think. I also keep hearing in my head your pronunciation of my name when you'd occasionally decide to say it in your nasally robot voice. And of course . . . your "CLOS U EYES" t-shirt. I can barely look at that thing or even think about it, actually, without falling apart.

So anyway . . . Ivan found this perfect place for us to have your memorial, I scanned photos nonstop for three days, and we got everything together somehow. That was a new kind of adrenaline for me . . . can't say I hated it, really . . . but I couldn't figure out what exactly to put in the memorial pamphlet. Of course I looked through all your computer files . . . I'm sorry about that . . . and through your email . . . I'm sorry about that too. But there was that "7 Things" thing you'd make everyone in your life fill out at some point. And I couldn't find your answers but I thought if anyone had them it would be your friend Shazzy. So I called her, I think, the night before the memorial, and she was like *If there's one thing your dad taught me, it's to always back your shit up!* And she fucking found it ... she found the answers to your "7 Things" thing. So I ended up making a nice memorial pamphlet out of that. It was a completely fucking perfect day, in the end. If you had anything to do with that, thank you. Apart from missing a few people, like you for instance, we had such a beautiful day, ate so much good food, drank so much brandy, looked at all those photos of you and listened to your favourite tunes ... Mom got all those orchids from the wholesaler or whatever ... I read that sweet and very embarrassing thing I'd written to help keep you out of jail that one time—"My Father, the Benign Being" ... no, I didn't explain the context ...

Then we came home and I just fully lost it. The guy had delivered your ashes to us the day before and I'd kind of fainted at that point, you know. So there you were ... in a bag in a cardboard box ... and I really couldn't deal with it. Ugh, sorry, I think I just need to make sure this camera's on again. It would really suck if this weren't recording ...

Wow, this is gonna run out soon ... we might need another tape! Actually I really have to pee. Just a sec ...

Hi! Sorry about that. It's so fucking cold in here.

Okay. So, yeah ... we cleaned up the hut ... there'd been this crazy sunset ... there's like kind of a full moon or something ... just a beautiful night. A couple of your friends had been too choked up to speak, but a handful of them had gone up and said such wonderful things about you, about eating with you and laughing with you and working with you ... how smart but stuck you were ... you know ...

So we drove home . . . I think a few of my closest friends came over . . . but I just grabbed your ashes and retreated to the bedroom and proceeded to scream my face off into your mattress. I remember staring so hard at your ashes, trying to process what I was seeing, what my sense perception was having to fucking deal with . . . god I'd be crying so hard right now if I weren't medicated. It's kind of weird but I guess it's a relief . . .

Then Christmas was a few days later and it was . . . well, total fucking crap. Kind of had a fight with Mom. It was hard for me to know how to help her and how to help myself at the same time. She must miss you so much too. You were the fucked-up centre of everything for both of us . . .

What else did I need to remember?

There's the fact that you'd somehow managed to pause *The Astronaut Farmer* . . . before you went to the gas station and then came home and died . . . you paused it right at this moment where Billy Bob Thornton's got the voice-over narrative about, like, one's relationship to one's dad. When you're a kid you wanna be just like him, when you're a teenager you want nothing to do with him, then when you're a grownup you realize you're just like him. Jesus fucking Christ . . . eventually Mom and I watched that movie and, yeah, were really feeling grateful for whatever tiny crumbs you were leaving us. Kinda spooky but, you know, very welcome.

I love you so much, Dad. And I didn't think I was ever going to feel better. And sometimes I don't—sometimes I feel just as bad. Sometimes, you know, I feel worse.

Oh god . . . then there was all the shit with you remembering the encounter with Moonface! That was really getting to you. Maybe

I'll meet that friend of yours in the spring, the friend who kinda compelled you into remembering—I hope you don't mind. I'm just sorry you didn't get a chance to speak on *Coast to Coast* . . . you were so excited about that. You were fucked up about it but happy to be making sense of who you were in relation to all that.

You know, every so often I'll get drunk and open up the little opal weed vessel and dig out the biggest piece of bone I can find and kind of bite on it, just like this . . .

I think we might be able to stick to one tape for tonight . . . what do you think? Six minutes left . . .

There's so much I love about you and need to remember about you. I miss you so much. You were, you know, my best friend . . . but you were in a lot of pain. You hated so many things. You loved me so much, but you hated so many things . . . I just don't know what it means that I will never be loved by anyone as much as you loved me.

I don't want you to worry about me. I don't want you to worry about my choices. I know what I'm doing, Dad. I'm going to be okay . . . just help me be healthy and not, you know . . . wander naked into the snow or whatever. Maybe I can talk to you like this more often. Or maybe I won't need to, which scares me.

Hail Atlantis!

Yeah, we listened to this song driving with your ashes to China Beach from the bed and breakfast in Sooke. Thank you for helping us figure out what to do that day . . . what to do with that portion of your ashes we'd brought along. We both didn't know and knew exactly what we were doing. I'm going back there at the beginning of January . . . we'll chat more then, I'm sure.

In the meantime . . . it'd be nice to see you in more of my dreams. Especially if I can see you a bit happier in more of my dreams, you know?

Maybe you could help me write my papers, too. Jeffrey "The Yellow Dart" Actis.

I miss you so much, Dad. But you're completely part of me. I think of you a million times a day, I hear your voice . . . eventually I'll figure out what parts of me need some kind of, you know, bigger differentiation from you . . . but who knows? Maybe I am exactly like you.

Thank you for everything, okay?

I just can't believe you died. It's really the fucking weirdest. I just can't believe you died on me. But I hope you're okay . . . I'm sure you are.

Oh shit! Sorry . . . your bones are really kinda crumbly.

Alright. Goodnight.

I'll just wait till it turns itself off, okay?

Yes, I'm going to eat a tiny sliver of your bone. Why not?

Fucking crazy. This is so insane. Just totally . . . pure sparkling dust.

DBT Workbook.

2. 1. Splitting
   2. try to flee (physically and/or emotionally)
   3. have the desire/need to self- (and other-) harm.

5. checked all 3 (but #1 less so)

7. 1. Increases worry about the future. Internalizes things that needn't be internalized. Shame.
   2. Feelings of loneliness emerge, like I will inevitably have to face everything on my own. Makes me believe that I can predict other people's behaviors/feelings and control them.
   3. Deceive myself into thinking that I am unlikeable and extreme, like people ~~can only~~ are only allowed to see either the really good or the really bad Andrea.
   4. Not so much to numb myself as to occasion the horrible possibility of letting demons out. Hangovers make it impossible for me to think about work/ideas. Compromises my self-image and makes me gain weight.
   5. That about sums it up. Guilt, disbelief, causing just as much grief for myself as for others. Getting older and worrying that good and beautiful people will stop coming into my life.
   6. Yup, all of those. Scaring and hurting people I love.
   7. Thankfully I don't [really] do this anymore.
   8. I guess I thought I'd dealt with the causes of my problems. Obviously there is still much hidden shit.

11. Radical acceptance coping statements:
"All the events have led up to now."
"I can't change what's already happened."
"The present is the only moment I have control over."

The Serious Angels: A True Story

1.

I tell how I came to think of writing a story about angels. I told my friend for whom I am writing this story that I would write a story for him about angels. When I said that, I did not mean either a true story, or not a true story. I was not thinking about anything in particular that had recently come to my knowledge about angels, or anything in particular that I had been recently imagining about angels. But suddenly it seemed to me that angels had been for a long time left out of people's conversation, as if there were no more angels, just as there are no more birds of certain kinds there used to be—or as if there had never been any angels, and people had invented them, for stories, and then grown tired of them. Suddenly I felt that angels ought to be brought back into people's conversation. I shall tell you why I felt so. My story—this story—was intended to be a story for a book of stories for children. In writing it I would be writing for children, talking to children: this fact made me feel more serious about my task than if it had been to write a story for grown-ups. For people expect you to write in a certain way when you write for children; and if you do your story will have some fooling in it, and if you don't your story will not seem a children's story. I had made up my mind to write in such a way that I could say to my readers about everything I said, "No fooling—I mean it!" I would have to watch myself, and not say anything that I could not say in perfect seriousness—that was, to my knowledge, not sensible, while spoken as if it were. Don't think I am against people's writing things for fun—for children's or grown-ups' fun, or their own. I am talking about *plain* stories. I was aiming at writing a plain story.

Now, grown-ups may not like my saying what I am going to say in front of children, in front of their children. But I have to say it, to explain my choosing angels for the subject of my story. Children, in much that they are given, are not given the best. It may seem to children that a good deal of what they get *is* the best. The toys are shiny or pretty or useful for passing time with. The stories written for them make them laugh, and feel sad, and then glad again, and take them in imagination to places and into houses strange to them, so that they feel that they know much more about the world than they see of it where they are. And what is said to them by grown-ups when they talk to them seriously, to help them understand the things of life better, is spoken, generally, with kindness, and with care to tell them no more than they think they can understand at their age, and only what they think will do them good at their age. Yet with the toys, and the stories, and the explanations of things, and with much else that is done for children, there is something lacking. What is given in them is not people's whole best, but a special best, a best specially invented for children, cut down from whole-best.

Both children and grown-ups would be better off if there were not these two different bests; there would be more of the whole best in people's lives—in the lives of children and of grown-ups too—if children were not given these little bests, children's bests, instead of *the* best. Most of what grown-ups give to one another for best is also a best cut down from whole-best. It is not so much cut down from whole best as children's best is, but it is not quite the same as whole-best. Grown-ups do not quite give one another the best they have to give, not quite. To illustrate what I mean I need only to point out how people talk to one another. This talk to one another is not much more careful or wise, or much more beautiful in its thoughts, than their talk to children. If they did their whole best in talking to children, they would be ashamed to do less in talking to one another. If they did their whole-best in talking to one another, they would be ashamed to do less in talking to children.

Now, I felt that if I told a story about angels for children, I should have the very best kind of beings for characters of my story. Whether people believe that there are such things as angels or not, they have to put their best ideas into their thought and their talk about them. For an angel is the very best kind of being that anyone could be. Whether you believe that there are or ever were such things as angels, or not, when you say the word 'angel', or think about such things as angels, you have to think about the best kind of being that could be. So, suddenly, I wanted to write a story about angels: I wanted a good subject, and there couldn't be a better subject. I won't say any more about my choosing this subject for a story. I hope that the story will make everything clear that I haven't yet made clear about how I feel about children, and grown-ups, and angels.

2.

I get ready to begin my story. And yet I find that I am not quite ready to begin my story. I feel a need to have you know me a little better before I begin my story. I feel that *you* need to know the author of *your* story a little better before you begin to read it. I want you to make you as much at home with me as possible, so that you shall not think of me as either

"The present moment is perfect, even if I don't like what's happening."

"This moment is exactly as it should be, given what's happened before it."

"This moment is the result of over a million other decisions."

"I am still a child and I am full of love and compassion that is rooted in being present."

"My soul might choose this for me. Accept my lesson and rise to its challenges."

"Everyone struggles but is fundamentally here and full of love."

12. Review a non-upsetting event that happened in your life many years ago, and use radical acceptance to remember the event without judging it.

My father died and I found his body.

Jody cheated on me because I drove him away.

I was often humiliated by my peers in elementary, middle, and high school.

I have hurt and scared many of the people who love me and who I love.

I have fled when I have not really wanted to flee.

I say things to people in order to hurt them as much as I'm hurting.

EXISTENTIALISM

5 senses experience ⟷ mental experiences

(but which is immanent and which is transcendent?
↳ maybe this needs to be revised/inverted)

• we can choose to move left on the spectrum @ any given moment

- not realistic to ~~try~~ expect to inhabit / sustain the zen experience ... not all / nothing

- existential authenticity is ambiguous, yet strives towards the ethical (negative / negating) Kantian "freedom"

  - aspirational
  - towards freedom, but suspended in the aesthetic.

OMG!

Ethics of Ambiguity

ETHIOPIAN FOOD!

If you're overwhelmed by the mental, at least make the choice to move left and take inventory. (Elastic (on) around the wrist ... a pet ... an ice cube)

fooling or preaching, but thinking my natural thoughts in what I tell and say. I should very much like you to feel at home in my story; so, I am trying to make you feel at home with me, for a start. I can well describe my feelings by comparing you with guests in a house where your host earnestly desires that you feel at home: no matter how much thought has been put into trying to make the house home-like for you, the first requirement for your feeling at home in it is that you feel at home with your host . . . Therefore, I am going to talk on a little more, before I begin my story.

To some people, as you know, the name of 'saints' is given. These are mostly people who suffer for their goodness, and so become to other people an example of goodness. It is thought that after their death, as beings made up all of spirit, they have powers to help the living, each a special power; and many people still pray to saints, asking their help. Some people pray to angels to do things for them. But that is almost like praying to someone in the same room with you. Saints are in heaven—are in heaven, if they are anywhere. But angels are everywhere—are everywhere if they are anywhere: they walk beside you, come and go freely between where you are and somewhere else, anywhere else—if they *are*. They have never been dead. They, too, are made up all of spirit, as saints are; but they have always been made up of spirit only—their bodies don't seem to be missing from them, as it seems with saints, when you think of them. Angels are the livest, the most quick-moving and quick-acting beings that can be thought of—besides being the very best kind of beings; this is why, when they are pictured in the mind or represented in actual pictures, they are given wings.

I have to admit to you that I have only very vague ideas about the characters of my story, at this point. Or, I should say, about what characters to have in it, and what to have happen in it. My title announces that this is going to be a *true* story. It has to be true to me. How could I otherwise do justice to my subject, and to my readers? I am not going to 'make up' the characters. I want to give my readers the very best, in characters. A made-up angel, though angels are the best kind of being imaginable, would be inferior to a real angel. All my angels will be real ones: they will be taken from life, and not changed. They will, indeed, be more real in my story than they were, or are, in life.

I must immediately explain that while, according to my ideas, angels are beings who have never died, who can't die, the people whose better-selves they are can die, and, as things have been going ever since there came to be people, do die. I can also help my readers to understand my story by explaining that when I say that my characters are taken from life, I only mean what people ordinarily mean by 'life'—that is everything up to death. But, truly, I think of life as something going on before death and after death. I believe that what is ordinarily meant by 'life' is a beginning-part of the life of a person; at least, I think that a person's life need not end at death. I also believe that it is not necessary to die in order to live beyond the beginning-part of life—or what is ordinarily called 'life'. To explain how I think a person could go from one part of life to the other part without dying I should have to speak of how I think angels and people are related. Much of this you will learn from my story. And, after I have finished my story, I shall try to fill in any blank spots that I think may be left in your understanding of my ideas about angels and people, and life and death. For the present, I shall just point to something I said a few minutes ago: I spoke of angels as being the better-selves of people. Keep that in mind, and it will help you to put your imagination to work in my story.

I won't give my characters their real names because some people, reading the story, might recognize them, and disbelieve what I tell of them, and want to argue with me, or feel obliged in the interest of truth to declare my story to be fanciful nonsense. I am not going to let myself be drawn into trying to prove my story to be true. The characters are real, and I shall describe them exactly as I know them. As to what happens in the story: some of what I shall tell—in fact, the larger part of what I shall have to tell—will be what I see happening when I look into the lives of my characters (be it on this side or the other side of death) with the eyes of my soul. But whether I am seeing with my ordinary sight or the sight of my soul, I shall tell you what I see, without any story-telling fooling: I shall speak truly.

Someone could say, "You are not speaking truly! *I* see this and this, not what you see." But, still, what I told would be true: it would be a true account of what I saw, and my story would be a true story, not a made-up story. I am *in* this story; it could be said that I myself am one of the characters. The life that I tell in my story is part of my life, and my life is part of it. This is how it is when things are seen with the eyes of the soul. Perhaps you will understand better what I mean by this if I confide to you, running ahead of my story, that I consider *souls* and *angels* to be things very like each other; having a soul and having an angel, or being a soul and being an angel, come very close, as I think of souls and angels. You have heard of people having angels, have you not—guardian angels? I think there is not much difference between leaving it to your soul to take care of you, to guide you into right and safe paths, and leaving it to your particular angel. Your soul, or your angel, needs to see more than you are seeing with your ordinary sight, to help you. I have made my soul, or my angel, my partner in my telling of this story.

Dr. Villalba DOGS - don't have a sense of time like ours...
A "hole in the weight of the past"

INTERPERSONAL GROUP.

- I tune out when people I don't trust — too much happiness / cheer (one possibility)...
- language / chatter → I both need it and need silence, Nothing, MINDFULNESS.
- anxiety about leaving... but realize that it's anxiety over feeling like a snob when I isolate myself.

cf. my work: → critical of people who read for content and not form
→ critical of people who want to flatten out antagonisms

↳ this is capitalism, but it's also... A fake kind of community. One that lacks exposure and vulnerability.

Dad's soup ... I can improve on the recipe and still keep him close

Parents' ability to fix everything is a double-edged sword. Some things shouldn't be fixed. Some love needs to be metered somehow so that it doesn't become anxious and/or avoidant attachment.

CHILLS
WORLD
DOMINATION
"SWISS STEAK"
salt + pepper
prepare rice for about a week's worth.
for stew, use only onions and carrots...
smaller pieces of meat ... make a roux!
add beef bouillion ... cook a long time,
add boiled potatoes.

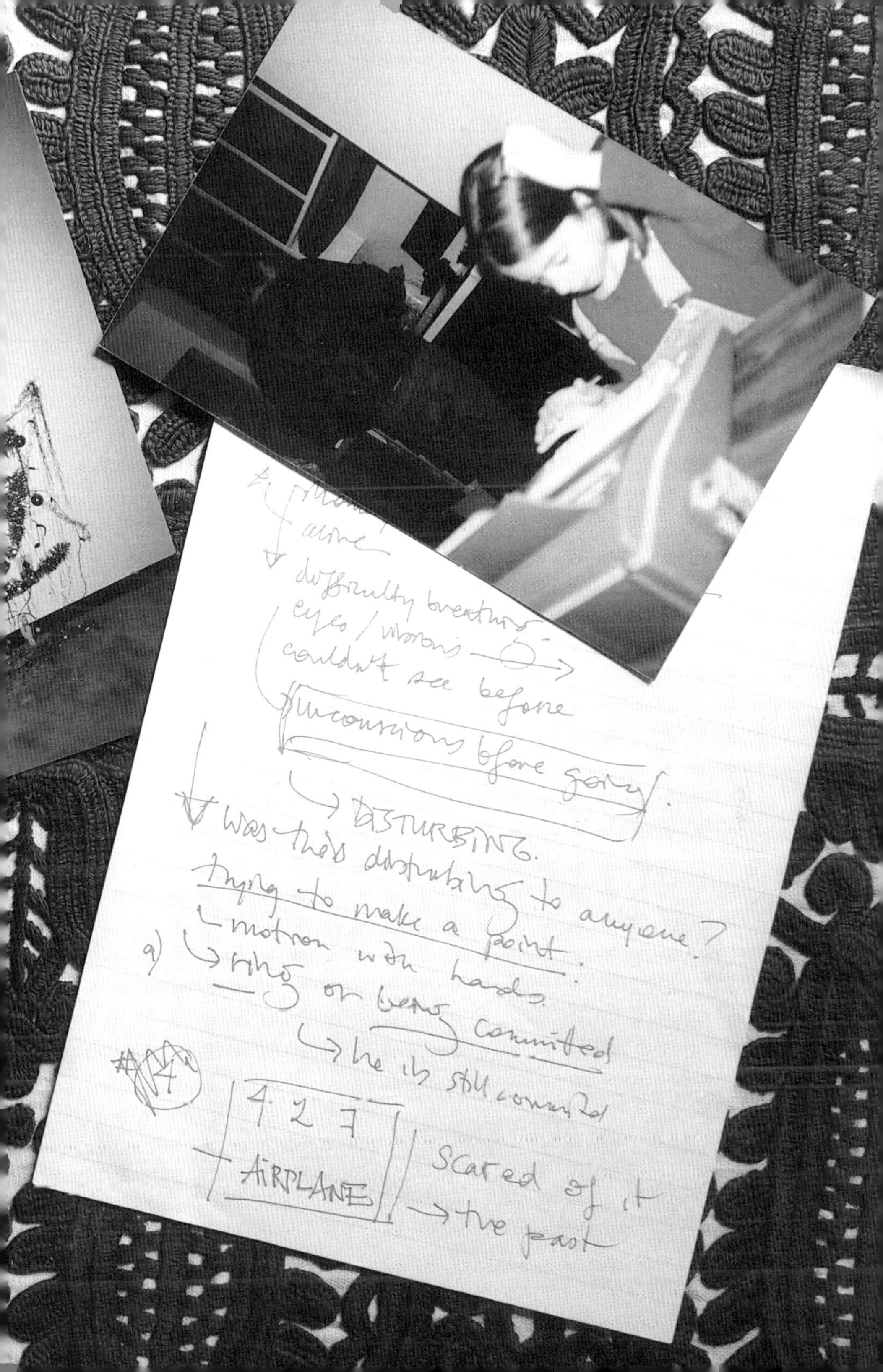

difficulty breathing
eyes / visions
couldn't see before
unconscious before going
DISTURBING.
Was this disturbing to anyone?
trying to make a point.
motion with hands.
ring or being committed
he is still committed
4 2 7
AIRPLANE
scared of it
the past

(no subject) Inbox ×

j. actis <greyallover@yahoo.com> Mon, Mar 5, 2007, 1:57 PM

to me

•••

GREY ALL OVER

Jeff where are ya? I need to ask you something.
From: Dave Barrow <davebarrow54@yahoo.ca>
To: Jeff Actis <greyallover@yahoo.com>
Date: 2007-07-07

How's it goin Jeff?
What ya been up to?
Did you get my facebook invite?
C'mon join up it's a hoot.
It's not too hard to figure out once you sign up.
Your ID is your email address.

Now this might seem like a weird question about our past, but I have to know if you remember this.

It definitely did happen!
I need to know if you remember this too.
It plagues me man.

Do you remember what you, I & Jim saw in the Rivercrest schoolyard when we were riding our bikes back from my house heading back over to Henley Cres?

You & Jim were riding double & I was on my bike.
I think you were on Jim's handlebars but it may have been the other way around.

We had just entered the school property at the Harefield end of the building and had just passed through the teachers' parking lot, coming up on turning the corner of the school to actually enter the schoolyard.
It was a summer evening about 8 pm give or take.
We were about 9 or 10 years old and we were riding really slow, gabbing away, when something we saw stopped us dead in our tracks. Whoever was on the handlebars actually jumped off and froze as did the rest of us.

Can you finish this memory Jeff?

I can tell you this...
I was over at your area hangin out with you & the guys on Henley almost every day of my childhood, every summer & weekend until dark or later for years and I walked or rode home through the schoolyard every night in the dark.

After we saw what we saw,
I didn't pass through that schoolyard for at least a year.
I just took the long way around.
Stayed on the roads.
That may be why I recall the incident so vividly.

Get back to me soon,
I've been dying to ask you this,

Your good pal,
Dave

Re: Jeff where are ya? I need to ask you something.
From: j. actis <greyallover@yahoo.com>
To: Dave Barrow <davebarrow54@yahoo.ca>
Date: 2007-07-09

Hi Dave,

Ok..you've got me really scratching my head over the schoolyard story?? I mean..do YOU know or remember what we saw? or are you asking me what we saw?

Was this before hallucinogens?
Please refresh my memory..

for now..

Jeff

Re: Jeff where are ya? I need to ask you something.
From: Dave Barrow <davebarrow54@yahoo.ca>
To: j. actis <greyallover@yahoo.com>
Date: 2007-07-10

Okay Jeff, I really wish you had of remembered this because you're really going to think I'm nuts now.
I'm far from being an artist but I tried a sketch & attached it to this email. I drew this from the point of view from behind our heads. We were facing west.

As I said we were riding along at a snail's pace, gabbing away as 10 year olds do, when this thing popped out from around the corner of the building and just stared at us.

DAVE

As I said we stopped dead and froze.

I saw this out of the corner of my eye.

It was about the same height as us which was probably about 3 or 4 ft tall.
It looked like another kid except its head was quite round and luminous.
There were no features except a hint of almost slit eyes and mouth, situated very close together which appeared as almost shadows. No hair. You know when you look at the full moon and it's very luminous but if you really look you can see some very light gray areas? Exactly like that!

I estimate this lasted about 30 seconds when it suddenly popped back behind the school out of sight.
The 3 of us looked at each other with a "What the hell was that?" look. Jumped back on the bikes with you back on Jim's bars and rode straight out of there, careful to make a very wide turn around that corner of the building so as not to get too close to it.
But as we rounded the corner we could see every inch of the entire schoolyard and there was no one to be seen. They had even taken the portables away so we had nothing obstructing our view.

We even slowly rode all along the back of the building checking every doorway and nook and nothing.

So what do ya think of that?
We were way to young for drugs then.

Dave

---

previous letter
From: Dave Barrow <davebarrow54@yahoo.ca>
To: Jeff Actis <greyallover@yahoo.com>
Date: 2007-07-14

Well Jeff,
By your lack of response, I would say you've written me off as some kind of nut.
I hope not, cuz I'm really not.
Anyways, hope you still email me once in a while,
I really get a blast talkin with ya.
Dave

Re: previous letter
From: j. actis <greyallover@yahoo.com>
To: Dave Barrow <davebarrow54@yahoo.ca>
Date: 2007-07-15

Dave,

Sorry to not reply until now..This is the busiest time of the year for me and most nights rather than drive home i just sleep on the boat that I'm working on..it's a long drive home and hardly seems worth the time driving.

Now..and get ready for this..

I honestly had no recollection of that night..zero..none..but now that has changed..dramatically. Your little sketch actually got my heart racing..and yes it did happen. I haven't stopped thinking of it since recalling it..and the image is now vivid in my mind. What i see in my mind's eye is this.. as you said..his head seemed to almost glow..like a light bulb was behind a translucent mask. And it was quite small...

guess we were also small at that time but I recall I thought it was smaller than us. It seemed a long time of silence staring at it...total silence. I remember that corner..I believe there was a little nook..like the brick wall protruded beyond the class room wall ..perhaps a yard or so? and it was from there that it appeared. As far as I remember.. there was no bright source of light in that area..like enough to illuminate that head in that way.

Dave.. what is for me very strange..and stranger than you can imagine..is my total loss of memory of this. As a matter of fact I was completely unaffected by this, and yet you were in enough fear to avoid that place for a long time. I don't recall remembering this event even right after it happened..like it never happened..but one would think a kid would be shaken up for a while and tell people about it. But I never did. Like it never happened. This I find very odd.

There were three of us, we all saw it, up close and focused, and it focused on us...and in this light, the only explanation for it was that we witnessed something unworldly.

What I really don't get is why it so quickly left my thoughts..totally completely..and it certainly shouldn't have. I have excellent long term memory (just don't ask about yesterday).. and yet this memory was gone..right up till i viewed your sketch.

Have you ever spoken of this to anyone else..? at least in your adult life? Ever ponder it in your mind over the years? Have you ever in your adult life..come to any conclusion about it?

I'll leave it at this for now. I don't have an answer.. but I'm not against the possibility of paranormal events. Pretty hard to not believe in the unbelievable when one has seen the unbelievable. Did you ever tell any family members, your mum or dad.. about it? I mean..at the time it happened?

If there's anything else you can add to the memory at all.. I mean following this event.. I would be interested to hear that.

And btw.. You're not nuts

Jeff

Wow
From: Dave Barrow <davebarrow54@yahoo.ca>
To: Jeff Actis <greyallover@yahoo.com>
Date: 2007-07-16

O God, Jeff!
You can't imagine the relief I'm feeling with you recalling this.
I was actually welling up reading your email.
I feel like 1000 lbs has been lifted off my head.
I feel positively fuckin joyous!
I know your not jerking my chain by your description which is dead on.
A light behind a mask...exactly!
That corner portrudes out about a yard from the classroom windows...absolutely true!
I had a feeling my little sketch might spark your memory.
After all a picture is worth 1000 words.
Okay, now I'm going to go have a smoke before I continue this note...

Okay I'm back!
I've thought about this every day of my life.
Every time I hear strange stories or theories of ghosts, goblins, ufos, aliens kidnapping people, inter dimensional travelers, I think to myself "Well that sounds pretty crazy but me and my friends we saw what we saw and it happened for sure, so who knows?"
Jeff I must get off to bed now and I'm going to have a good sleep because you remember.

I'll continue tomorrow,
I still have a lot to say,
Dave

---

quick note
From: Dave Barrow <davebarrow54@yahoo.ca>
To: Jeff Actis <greyallover@yahoo.com>
Date: 2007-07-17

sorry Jeff,
it's been crazy around here,
explain later.
I never mentioned it to anyone until my daughter about 10 years ago when we were watching a move, "fire in the sky"...a supposedly true story.
I just told my sister Sylvie the other day after getting your confirmation.
I have a theory as to your memory lapse...
and I'll bet Jim wouldn't remember either.
2 hours after seeing it I was faced with the fear of going home in the dark, thru the schoolyard again and it was still fresh in my mind,
anyways,
I have to dash off to work now,
will follow up asap,
Dave

---

follow up
From: Dave Barrow <davebarrow54@yahoo.ca>
To: Jeff Actis <greyallover@yahoo.com>
Date: 2007-07-20

Ok Jeff,
sorry for taking so long,

as I said things have been crazy around here the past couple of days & I haven't even had time to go on the computer.
plus, I have to share computer time with 3 other people at this time which I'll explain later.
but, as I start work at 6am today, I have a few minutes of solitude to write.

I've given this incident a lot of thought the past many years & a lot of questions have plagued me.
1st and foremost in my mind was "Do Jeff & Jim remember?"
We never really discussed it, not even right after it happened.
We didn't even know if we saw the same thing as each other.
I found this very strange for three 9 or 10 year old friends who always discussed or pondered life all the time.

2nd, where did "moonface" go?
We were right on his tail as soon as he popped back around the corner.
We could see the whole yard as we rounded the corner & checked every doorway & nook & cranny as we quickly rode along trying to get another glimpse.
I even remember scanning the rooftop as people always went on the school roof.
Though he probably had no time to get up there so fast.
Well I must get going again, time for work.
Will get back to you as soon as I can but it is a little difficult sometimes as I said. Attached a photo of me & my dog Maya taken Monday.
Dave

---

some more thoughts on the subject
From: Dave Barrow <davebarrow54@yahoo.ca>
To: Jeff Actis <greyallover@yahoo.com>
Date: 2007-07-20

Jeff, another quick note. It occurred to me that if this being had the ability to make people forget seeing him, then it stands to reason that this type of sighting of these beings may happen all the time, but nobody remembers the incidents.

Case in point, 99.9% of so called Alien abductions of people, that I'm sure you've heard about, are only recalled thru regressive hypnosis if you want to believe that sort of thing. Nevertheless, it is an interesting thought with regards to our incident.

I'm not suggesting that our "moonface" guy is of UFO origin as we never had any reason to believe that. But, have you ever seen a hypnotist at work?

I participated as a hypnosis test subject performed by a Psycologist who worked for the Workmens Compensation Board.
He told me that there were 9 tests hypnotists perform to test a subject's susceptibility to being hypnotized. Of which hypnotically induced amnesia was one.
It's the one test that didn't work on me.
Interesting eh?

Okay guy , I have to go to work, catch ya later,
Dave

Re: some more thoughts on the subject
From: j. actis <greyallover@yahoo.com>
To: Dave Barrow <davebarrow54@yahoo.ca>
Date: 2007-07-21

Dave..
i told my daughter about this.. i actually showed her our correspondence..

I don't know why..but i've always had this affinity with these things.. greyallover doesnt refer to my colour.. (well sometimes I'm covered in paint from work!).. and my previous address was url_grey (forgot the password to that account) so it is now greyallover again

anyway.. andrea says a long time ago i told her i saw something when i was a kid.. again i don't remember this~~~~ very frustrating

so...it was 40 years ago...i know it happened.. it was very strange.. i guess the next question would be does Jim remember? and if he does? then what?

if my daughter says i told her about this then i did.. just wish i had recall on this.

it's 40 degrees here and I'm going to Superstore and hope i never think about this again :)
hope all is going ok
cheers
Jeff

Re: some more thoughts on the subject
From: Dave Barrow <davebarrow54@yahoo.ca>
To: j. actis <greyallover@yahoo.com>
Date: 2007-07-21

Jeff, I guess I may have overwhelmed you a bit with my theories.
Too much to fast?
Sorry about that but Geez, I had a long time to mull this over and it's so great to have someone who remembers this unusual incident as well.
I contacted Jim about the same time as I did you.
He sent me a pleasant reponse and then I sent him the note that I also sent you done in MS Word about our childhood adventures.

I never heard back from him since, however I know he's a pretty busy guy these days as he indicated in his original response.
We are supposed to get together someday for a coffee or beer or something.
We only live about 25 minutes from each other but you know how times slips by. I mean look at us, 35 years or so slipped by.
Hey, I think it's great you've confided in Andrea.
It's really wonderful to have that kind of relationship with her isn't it?
I mean especially when you hear of some of the crappy relationships other parents have with their kids.
My kids are great like that too.
We're a couple of very fortunate old buggers eh?
Well off to bed for this guy,
Catch you in the next letter,
Dave

Obsessed
From: j. actis <greyallover@yahoo.com>
To: Dave Barrow <davebarrow54@yahoo.ca>
Date: 2007-07-27

Hi Dave..

Well, I have to say this,,tell this to someone.
Frankly, I'm going a little crazy here I think. Thing is, all of this new memory of the incident is eating me up. If I get more than 5 idle minutes during the day, then my thoughts are of nothing but that night. This is also complemented with it consuming my thoughts at night in bed. Remember, for me, the whole event just happened *now*..not forty years ago. I have to now make some sense of it all, and I've not the benefit of it happening forty years ago.

I'm not as concerned about seeing this thing.. more on the effect this encounter had. Do you have any memory of a *feeling* that you can't quite put a finger on.. like perhaps an emotion of some sort that you don't understand? or like you can't relate to any of the normal human emotions? We have all felt love and hate and fear and jealousy etc.. but what about feelings we don't have words for? Do you like me have a feeling this thing was of great intelligence? like enough to look at us and assure us there was nothing to fear? Why in the hell was I not scared..and why did it not occur to us to tell anyone.. even discuss it amongst the three of us.. ever again?

I cant help thinking that the only way for it to disappear so quickly, without a trace, was that it actually had plenty of time to make its escape as we lost sense of time, and as far as we knew, what we thought was mere seconds before we cornered the wall was actually much more time-- sort of like a déjà vu in reverse. Man~~~ I don't know.. like whats more believable to logic.. that a physical, living thing could disappear like that in seconds, or this living thing had some ability to put us into some kind of trance and we lost time .. maybe more than a minute.. or an hour or whatever.. Both ideas are so crazy, unless one totally accepts that what we saw was not of this world and thus, not of the same rules of this world.

As you can see here, I'm a bit obsessed with all of this right now, and although I know I'll never get an explanation, it will occupy me for a very long while I think. You've had all of these years to mull over this event, to at least try to make a comfortable sense of it, but for me, well this event just happened. I understand you saying "it plagues me" in your letter.. a good description for me now also.

You didn't mention if Jim replied specifically if he remembers that evening? I really hope I'm not the only one feeling this thing did something to me..something I can't even explain but I know is there.

Anyway, We're still in this horrible heatwave here and I need to get outside.

later,
Jeff

Re: Obsessed
From: Dave Barrow <davebarrow54@yahoo.ca>
To: j. actis <greyallover@yahoo.com>
Date: 2007-07-27

Hi Jeff,
I don't think this moonface guy actually did anything to us as much as the whole experience made everything we ever learned or were taught seem a little, well, two dimensional or bland or incomplete by comparison.
Our minds have been opened up to the super natural.
I mean geez...what we experienced was so out of our realm of possibilities.
Does that make sense what I just said?

I can truly understand what you're going thru.
As you said it's as though it just happened.It must be all so overwhelming.
But I must warn you, you'll feel the same way 5 or 10 or even 20 years from now.
The problem I've had is, even if I'd confided in someone about this incident and they really sincerely wanted to understand and believe... they really can't fathom the whole experience. The feelings and emotions that go along with it that you and I feel deep down inside
I guess that's why I was so emotional when you remembered.
Finally, someone who really really knows.

What vibe do I recall getting from this "moonface" character as we stood and faced each other?
I did not get a particularly warm feeling...I can tell you that.
I'll never forget the vibe I got...utter disregard, like the way a scientist might look at a lab rat or when a guy puts the bolt thru the head of a cow at Canada Packers might regard one of hundreds of cows a day.
I recall "moonguy's" expression as completely serious and he was just looking us over for who knows what reason. But I feel we didn't fit the bill, so to speak. Thank God!
That's probably why I was so scared to go thru that schoolyard for such a long time. I don't know if I mentioned it but that included daytime...if I was alone.

I'm sorry if I'm freaking you out Jeff, but I'm just being completely honest. This has really affected my whole life y'know.

Over the past 40 odd years since that happened, I've always paid particular attention to details of strange stories in print, on the radio or on television and movies always looking for similarities to our experience.
There really hasn't been much, but once in a while some minor detail of some reported experience will get my attention.
I won't bother you with all that now but let me know when you want to hear more.

I do find some comfort in this though.
But as I said there really hasn't been much in the way of figuring it all out.

Okay I must go now,
Take care Jeff.

Dave

```
0.475 kg @ $3.70/kg
 GRN SWT PEPPER           SCALE   1.76
 LARGE EGGS                       2.38
 PORK ROAST                       8.38
 BLADE STEAK                      2.48
 BLADE STEAK                      3.87
                                 ---------
      6% GST 122235922             1.43
      7.0% PST                     1.59
                                 ---------
      Balance Due                 97.61
0.225 kg @ $5.03/kg    25 g Tare
 MUSHROOMS WHITE          SCALE   1.13
 FM 2% MILK                       1.36
 GROUND BEEF                      2.86
                                 ---------
      6% GST 122235922             1.43
      7.0% PST                     1.59
                                 ---------
      Balance Due                102.96

 ======= TRANSACTION RECORD =======
 GLOBAL PAYMENTS MERCHANT M00845776
 The Real Canadian Superstore
 3185 Grandview Highway
 Vancouver BC
 STORE 1520        TERM L0152006
 SLIP 0009         REG 06
```

My kind of seriousness, in my looking to poetry for the rescue of human life from the indignities it was capable of visiting upon itself, led me to an eventual turning away from it as failing my kind of seriousness.

—Laura (Riding) Jackson

A clown dons a suit and reads an autopsy. A clown fakes a disappearance, in his clown suit, reading an autopsy. A death clown "plays," while doctors and poets and poet doctors and doctor clowns and clown poets argue about "art." Some people point at the clown, the autopsy he has cut up, clutched in his hand. The clown cries big fake tears that drip and soak his clown suit. The scissors still sharp and hidden in his suit. The makeup smears down his face, gets all over the doctors trying to soak them up with their sleeves. Others wait for him to melt.

—Oki Sogumi

CONTENTS

VOLTA: ONE POEM

I'd had two options:
a) kill myself;
b) kill myself.
I went for neither option and instead
listened to certain poets and people
listened especially closely
to what they were telling about
the State and its epic historical distortions of
miracle.
Believe it or not
this is all it took—
being shown how exactly
precisely
stupid we've always been
to let the State fuck up our
knowing better
about miracle.
The need to kill myself
could now become, at least
more about people
very much more about
things I could see.
Phew!

So what could I see
at that point
you ask?
Pretty much not anything
but the time:
it was time-for-a-whole-new-lighting-system o'clock.
True, there'd been trauma.
I had ignorance from some parts of it.
But I loved my ignorance
like I loved my old kind of need
to kill myself
and my old kind of need
to kill everyone if possible
by making my categories
a little bit more fascinating than theirs
my ancestors' noise
the louder of voices.
I'd always been quick to laughter
quick to cackle, I mean
so usually nobody could tell
what a bad witch
I was, only how badly I wanted to be
a good witch.

Then a different measurement for good seeing came along
which is exactly the wrong way to put it.
It didn't "come along"
unless you want the old kind of miracle
to start doing the talking again.
But how did I take notice, then?
As fucked up as simplicity is
it was fucking simple.
It involved a stopping.
Not a suicide
but that's how it tricks you
"it" being your old self
always thinking it's your new self
all ready to die
for the kinds of sins
that your sinning actually fails
to adequately
comprehend.
It involved
as I started to see in my stopping
angels that were literal
angels that are literal.
Integrated. Moving.

Do you remember when you didn't know you were racist?
Can you predict
how that question
is going to tie into the matter of this
one poem?
You don't have to know for sure
but you for sure
have to feel it.
I'd understood difference
when I arrived.
Sensed my knowing was as pale
as my pain was unshareable.
Spiriting my way
in and out of AA
which are my own initials
I wrote poetry only
when I felt extremely jealous.
No ideas, back then
but in aggression.
How fearfully I'd loved
the wrong ways of loving
and made of my dancing
asphyxiated play.

To be honest, this is the first time
I've written a poem and been
able to hear myself saying something inside of it.
In listening, my own
exactitude takes shape.
Unmiraculously.
This isn't a prize or a price.
We are labouring together
even though I owe you.
The fearlessness might be
surplus itself.
We will keep renaming everything.
I will keep fucking up.
I will keep not killing myself
for fucking up; instead
I will quietly grow loud
and finally learn to drive
so I can wait for you in the car
as you're stealing your things back
to take us wherever
we need to go.
It will be
a better here, but here.

LVII

EXCEPT the heaven had come so near,
So seemed to choose my door,
The distance would not haunt me so;
I had not hoped before.

But just to hear the grace depart
I never thought to see,
Afflicts me with a double loss;
'T is lost, and lost to me.

PHYLLIS WEBB
WATER AND LIGHT
SELECTED POEMS
HANGING FIRE
PHYLLIS WEBB
LASZLO

2018–09–06

22:00

Stoned on funny gummy and listening to dark side of the Mona cuz it's your 64th birthday. A semi-}{'austere d version of it comes up in Spotify, I listen to, dance a little maksome snacks, then frigging brothers on arms (the actually song not the whole Alvin,,, the song Marti dances tonin the one videok(. It comes ON and I am eating melted cheese and Elgin holy shit I go over to see if it was on a playlist or somebutbbut NO not even Song radio. Just out of nowhere tat song comes on, no trace of a thing except LOTS of a gost!

22:10

Snacking my fixing brains out because apparently I didn't stuff enough food in my face at x-site earlie. Tata and mom met me there after I'd spent an hour on this book feeling nice but also very guilty for spending your birthday night appropriating shirt from your journall trying to say things about the inadequacy of certain lenses n orientations and of curs e drinking the poison that killed you!. Nachosish now as "in your eyes" comes on and I wonder if I will accidentally set my new apsoarment on fire..

22:20

Had my second day of classes today and it guess it's true I am a teachijerx. Found myself sumantenaouy snappy and way too friendly for the most part. Little Boss "objcctive summary" //"care package" clown laughing too readily for u as usual...here comet o my office nad eat all my trukish delight while we'res at it.You'd laugh so hard at me..

22:30

Oh man, that Eric Clapton's motherless child song is on and I remember the movie I first heard this in with cancer'd Laura linney and kevin spacey, how they dance sexy soulful to it I think after she decides to stop getting all treatments., how it was the first time I was like for SURE let me die not-suddenly/unexpredlu, please give me at least some months and this one last dance with John spaced to this catchy Clapton track that, you know, when I finally looked it up just has the worst lyrics about mistreating women then he uses his abandonment issues to do violent things to his girl. Doesn't know right from wrong yeah well I guess you fucking ARE motherless

22:40

KING crimson from wherrrree??? in this moment. More straight up mentor cheese. So ducking tired but determined to make the most of this one evening of stoned cuommunion. I feel like I haven't had a new creative idea (except about myself identitywise) in years actually..,maybe revising my dfW Chapter from violenctly reverent/ proselytizfnig/apologist to "how did we settttle for this!!" As truth or seriousness or of what have you...How AA which are my own initials was what made me like his writing mostly but this was before I even (almost accidentally_discovered how to adequately reject. Him. And throw out the part of me that fell for that kin dof clown....? to become instead my own kind of closn (see above))-- as well as a better listenger and more trusting of the fierrence betwwn wholly serious and limtitedly serious angerss.. He's still somewhere in me probably though --like YOU, haha!

22:50

How it was ecxactly NOT drinking for half a year six years ago that made me first take wholyy seriuosly the slinozajst principle of substance monism intuitive science no accidents except sure there is HISTROY and you mst consider it and bear it and fight it and what ave you . . . . >fuck I was going to make that video art ojbect of Marti Tata mom right brefore Martu got sick where we sit at their big table in Burquitslam and I mansplain Spinoza tonthem. Woulbe been like wht I am now---hi " I'm-a-funeral-director pretending to be your son's english professor.."tryna to bring a shareable wisdom and a comfort and knowledge of okayness also. responsiblilty/anger alsp. What if god was one of us? Just a slab like one of us? etcc..

23:00

What isf god was both creative nnd uncreative

23:10

but mostly creative

23:20

What if god was exactly your kind of seriousness

23:30

What if god was exactly OUR kinf of seriusness

23:40

What if "Miracles only seem to be new owing to men's ignorance"

23:50

Wht if we tested every idea by always and exactly invtenging a new nest/?

00:00

What if seriuofness saved lives??

CLOS
U
EYES

SEVEN THINGS

Seven things that scare me . . .

1. water snakes
2. getting exploded
3. not knowing how to tell it or help it
4. being in the way
5. being hated
6. being loved
7. death still somehow

Seven things that make me laugh . . .

1. death still somehow
2. being tickled obviously
3. extraterrestrial drug
4. the night we called in for the miracle water
5. the butt-turd-toast joke
6. virtually all memes
7. lemons4ever@hotmail.com

Seven things I love . . .

1. doing things quietly
2. doing things exactly
3. the movie *Photographing Fairies*
4. my mom a.k.a. the spirit of dance
5. fruiting bodies
6. whole seriousness
7. death still somehow

Seven things I loathe . . .

1. death still somehow
2. limited seriousness
3. not telling the difference
4. my belatedness
5. shit readings of Spinoza
6. collegial fuddy-duddies
7. basically any false prophet

Seven things I don't understand . . .

1. fiction
2. yachts
3. non-trauma
4. what to do or not do with "4 2 7"
5. how to build a normal argument
6. déjà vu in reverse
7. death still somehow

35 As Above/So Below

Seven things on my desk . . .

1. *Surviving Death*
2. just a little candle
3. baby peyote from Dylan
4. Sally Hansen Miracle Gel in "Greyfitti"
5. paper paper paper
6. "You are soon going to change your present line of work" fortune
7. Jeffrey Mona Marti

Seven things I am right now . . .

1. 35
2. nervous/careful
3. waiting for endo surgery
4. in debt
5. indebted
6. eyes/vision good
7. future death doula?

Seven somewhat unknown facts about me . . .

1. I accept Christmas
2. easy A
3. I have no good underwear
4. I have a giant Moonface tattoo on my back
5. who cares
6. I've shared all my facts already
7. despite all my wrath I'm still just a people pleaser hatched in the Year of the Rat

Seven things to do before I die . . .

1. relax
2. do *not* relax
3. abandon normal arguments
4. make Whitley Strieber read my book
5. be a grandmother
6. tell it and help it
7. death still somehow

NOTES

Most of the written texts in this book are (or emerge from) transcriptions of files in my iPhone Notes app or of audio/video recordings created between 2007 and 2018.

Thank you to Dylan Godwin for the title of the book's opening sequence, "Soul Ash." Thank you to *The Capilano Review* for publishing "Soul Ash" in its Summer 2020 issue (*TCR* 3.41).

Thank you to my mom, Katalin Actis, for allowing me to publish our conversation in "2007-12-14." Thank you to my dad's childhood best friend for his extremely generous permission to include the email correspondence and his sketch of Moonface in "Grey All Over." At Dave's request, I have changed his surname.

Page 9: Scribing image is reproduced with permission from Rev. Dr. Janice L. Dreshman, Registered Lily Dale Medium, Lily Dale, NY.

Pages 88-91: "Description of a Struggle" first appeared in the group show Less is More: The Poetics of Erasure (SFU Galleries, 2008, curated by Bill Jeffries and Ariana Kelly) and subsequently in *The Capilano Review* Winter 2009 issue (*TCR* 3.7). Language is borrowed from Franz Kafka's early short story "Description of a Struggle," translated by Tania and James Stern (in *The Complete Stories*, Schocken, 1971).

Pages 111, 112, 115, and 116: Excerpt taken from Laura (Riding) Jackson's "The Serious Angels: A True Story" (1966), first published in *Chelsea* 69 (2000): *The Sufficient Difference: A Centenary Celebration of Laura (Riding) Jackson.* Thank you to Elizabeth Friedmann, the issue's guest editor and (Riding) Jackson's biographer, for always taking my work on (Riding) Jackson seriously, and to the Division of Rare and Manuscript Collections, Cornell University Library, for permission to reproduce these pages.

Page 138: Epigraphs taken from (Riding) Jackson's introduction to *The Poems of Laura Riding* (Persea Books, 1980, p. xi) and from Oki Sogumi's contribution to "Kenneth Goldsmith Says He Is an Outlaw" (June 1, 2015), compiled by CAConrad for the Poetry Foundation's *Harriet Blog* in response to Goldsmith's performance of "The Body of Michael Brown" at Brown University on March 13, 2015.

Page 145: Scanned page is from (Riding) Jackson's copy of *The Complete Poems of Emily Dickinson* (M. Secker, 1928), held in the Division of Rare and Manuscript Collections at Cornell University Library. Image reproduced with permission.

Page 157: Line borrowed from the "On miracles" chapter of Benedict de Spinoza's *Theological-Political Treatise* (1670), edited by Jonathan Israel and translated by Israel and Michael Silverthorne (Cambridge University Press, 2007, p. 95).

Pages 163-64: Penny Slinger, "As Above / So Below" card from the Secret Dakini Oracle Tantric Divination Deck (1979) © Penny Slinger / SOCAN (2020). Used with permission. Thanks to CAConrad for sharing this beloved tarot deck with us during their visit to Vancouver in May 2016.

Page 167: Arbitrary rhinocerous stationery © Small World Unlimited (1971).

THANKS

Thank you to everyone who has helped me feel safe, supported, sexy, or otherwise alive and enlivened over the last dozen years in both my writing and my non-writing. Thank you especially to Rebecca Brewer, Peter Bussigel, Natalie Knight, Dylan Godwin, Jordan Scott, Aisha Sasha John, Ada Smailbegović, Danielle LaFrance, Coleman Nye, Mariko Molander, Trevor Shikaze, Matthew McBride, HaeAhn Kwon, Paul Kajander, Tim Terhaar, John Mac Kilgore, Anick Rolland, Broc Rossell, Lara LeMoal, Luke Rogers, Sarah Osment, Michael Conboy, Laura Fisher, Swetha Regunathan, Stefanie Sevcik, and Jeffrey Neilson. And thank you to Adam Alic, a serious angel with whom this is my life now.

For their presence and actions in the earliest hours and days of my grief, thank you to Denise Oleksijczuk, Stephen Collis, Ivan Drury, and Stacey Bishop. For intervening a few years later, thank you to everyone at the Rhode Island Hospital Adult Partial Program, especially Dr. Lindsey Anderson, and to anyone at Brown University who didn't make me feel like a fucking alien.

For encouraging me in the making and sharing of my manuscript, thank you to Aisha (again), Jordan (again), Jenny Penberthy, Listen Chen, Mallory Amirault, CAConrad, Tiziana La Melia, Matea Kulić, and Fenn Stewart. Thank you to Monroe Lawrence, Trevor (again), and Adam (again) for their careful feedback at important and stressful moments of the editing process. Thank you to Aisha (again), Sachiko Murakami, and Jen Currin for their blurbs and of course for their very whole seriousness.

Thank you to everyone at Brick Books, especially Alayna Munce, Cara-Lyn Morgan, Nick Thran, River Halen Guri, Kitty Lewis,

Brenda Leifso, and my editor, John Barton. John, you're a miraculous reader and I'll forever be grateful to have had your eyes and your heart on this project.

And thank you, above/below all, to my parents and grandparents: Katalin, Jeffrey, Marta, and Stefan. I'm blessed to have landed in your complicated lives and loving arms.

Andrea Actis was born in Toronto but for most of her life has lived in Vancouver on the unceded territories of the Musqueam, Squamish, and Tsleil-Waututh Nations. She teaches writing and literature at Capilano University and from 2015–17 edited *The Capilano Review*. *Grey All Over* is her first book.